THE VIOLENT BEAR IT AWAY

- character seeking to assume role of prophet + to bring himself into a better relationship w/ GOD

BOOKS BY

Flannery O'Connor

NOVELS

Wise Blood

The Violent Bear It Away

STORIES

A Good Man Is Hard to Find

Everything That Rises Must Converge
with an introduction by Robert Fitzgerald

The Collected Stories of Flannery O'Connor
edited and with an introduction
by Robert Giroux

NON-FICTION

Mystery and Manners
edited and with an introduction
by Robert and Sally Fitzgerald

The Habit of Being
edited and with an introduction
by Sally Fitzgerald

"FROM THE DAYS OF JOHN THE BAPTIST UNTIL NOW, THE KINGDOM OF HEAVEN SUFFERETH VIOLENCE, AND THE VIOLENT BEAR IT AWAY." Matthew 11:12

THE VIOLENT BEAR IT AWAY

FLANNERY O'CONNOR

Farrar, Straus & Giroux   *New York*

Twentieth printing, 1988

For Edward Francis O'Connor
1896-1941

ONE

I

FRANCIS MARION TARWATER'S uncle had been dead for only half a day when the boy got too drunk to finish digging his grave and a Negro named Buford Munson, who had come to get a jug filled, had to finish it and drag the body from the breakfast table where it was still sitting and bury it in a decent and Christian way, with the sign of its Saviour at the head of the grave and enough dirt on top to keep the dogs from digging it up. Buford had come along about noon and when he left at sundown, the boy, Tarwater, had never returned from the still.

The old man had been Tarwater's great-uncle, or

said he was, and they had always lived together so far as the child knew. His uncle had said he was seventy years of age at the time he had rescued and undertaken to bring him up; he was eighty-four when he died. Tarwater figured this made his own age fourteen. His uncle had taught him Figures, Reading, Writing, and History beginning with Adam expelled from the Garden and going on down through the presidents to Herbert Hoover and on in speculation toward the Second Coming and the Day of Judgment. Besides giving him a good education, he had rescued him from his only other connection, old Tarwater's nephew, a schoolteacher who had no child of his own at the time and wanted this one of his dead sister's to raise according to his own ideas.

The old man was in a position to know what his ideas were. He had lived for three months in the nephew's house on what he had thought at the time was Charity but what he said he had found out was not Charity or anything like it. All the time he had lived there, the nephew had secretly been making a study of him. The nephew, who had taken him in under the name of Charity, had at the same time been creeping into his soul by the back door, asking him questions that meant more than one thing, planting traps around the house and watching him fall into them, and finally coming up with a written study of him for a schoolteacher magazine. The stench of his behaviour had reached heaven and the Lord Himself had rescued the old man. He had sent him a rage of vision, had told him to fly with the orphan boy to the farthest part of the backwoods and raise him up to justify his Redemption. The Lord had assured him a long life and he had snatched the baby from under the schoolteacher's nose and taken him to live in the clearing, Powderhead, that he had a title to for his lifetime.

The old man, who said he was a prophet, had raised the boy to expect the Lord's call himself and to be prepared for the day he would hear it. He had schooled him in the evils that befall prophets; in those that come from the world, which are trifling, and those that come from the Lord and burn the prophet clean; for he himself had been burned clean and burned clean again. He had learned by fire.

He had been called in his early youth and had set out for the city to proclaim the destruction awaiting a world that had abandoned its Saviour. He proclaimed from the midst of his fury that the world would see the sun burst in blood and fire and while he raged and waited, it rose every morning, calm and contained in itself, as if not only the world, but the Lord Himself had failed to hear the prophet's message. It rose and set, rose and set on a world that turned from green to white and green to white and green to white again. It rose and set and he despaired of the Lord's listening. Then one morning he saw to his joy a finger of fire coming out of it and before he could turn, before he could shout, the finger had touched him and the destruction he had been waiting for had fallen in his own brain and his own body. His own blood had been burned dry and not the blood of the world.

Having learned much by his own mistakes, he was in a position to instruct Tarwater—when the boy chose to listen—in the hard facts of serving the Lord. The boy, who had ideas of his own, listened with an impatient conviction that he would not make any mistakes himself when the time came and the Lord called him.

That was not the last time the Lord had corrected the old man with fire, but it had not happened since he had taken Tarwater from the schoolteacher. That time his rage of vision had been clear. He had known what he was saving the boy from and it was saving and not destruction he was seeking. He had learned enough to hate the destruction that had to come and not all that was going to be destroyed.

Rayber, the schoolteacher, had shortly discovered where they were and had come out to the clearing to get the baby back. He had had to leave his car on the dirt road and walk a mile through the woods on a path that appeared and disappeared before he came to the corn patch with the gaunt two-story shack standing in the middle of it. The old man had been fond of recalling for Tarwater the red sweating bitten face of his nephew bobbing up and down through the corn and behind it the pink flowered hat of a welfare-woman he had brought along with him. The corn was planted up to four feet from the porch that year and as the nephew came out of it, the old man appeared in the door with his shotgun and shouted that he would shoot any foot that touched his step and the two stood facing each other while the welfare-woman bristled out of the corn, ruffled like a peahen upset on the nest. The old man said if it hadn't been for the welfare-woman, his nephew wouldn't have taken a step. Both their faces were scratched and bleeding from thorn bushes and a switch of blackberry bush hung from the sleeve of the welfare-woman's blouse.

She had only to let out her breath slowly as if she were releasing the last patience on earth and the nephew lifted his foot and planted it on the step and the old man shot him in the leg. He recalled for the boy's benefit the nephew's expression of outraged righteousness, a look that had so infuriated him that he had raised the gun slightly higher and shot him again, this time taking a wedge out of his right ear. The second shot flushed the righteousness off his face and left it blank and white, revealing that there was nothing underneath it, revealing, the old man sometimes admitted, his own failure as well, for he had tried and failed, long ago, to rescue the nephew. He had kidnapped him when the child was seven and had taken him to the backwoods and baptized him and instructed him in the facts of his Redemption, but the instruction had lasted only for a few years; in time the child had set himself a different course. There were moments when the thought that he might have helped the nephew on to his new course himself became so heavy in the old man that he would stop telling the story to Tarwater, stop and stare in front of him as if he were looking into a pit which had opened up before his feet.

At such times he would wander into the woods and leave Tarwater alone in the clearing, occasionally for days, while he thrashed out his peace with the Lord, and when he returned, bedraggled and hungry, he would look the way the boy thought a prophet ought to look. He would look as if he had been wrestling a wildcat, as if his head were still full of the visions he had seen in its eyes, wheels of light and strange beasts with giant wings of fire and four heads turned to the four points of the universe. These were the times that Tarwater knew that when he was called, he would say, "Here I am, Lord, ready!" At other times when there was no fire in his uncle's eye and he spoke only of the sweat and stink of the cross, of being born again to die, and of spending eternity eating the bread of life, the boy would let his mind wander off to other subjects.

The old man's thought did not always move at the same rate of speed through every point in his story. Sometimes, as if he did not want to think of it, he would speed over the part where he shot the nephew and race on, telling how the two of them, the nephew and the welfare-woman (whose very name was comical—Bernice Bishop) had scuttled off, making a disappearing rattle in the corn, and how the welfare-woman had screamed, "Why didn't you tell me? You knew he was crazy!" and how when they came out of the corn on the other side, he had noted from the upstairs window where he had run that she had her arm around the nephew and was holding him up while he hopped into the woods. Later he learned that he had married her though she was twice his age and he could only possibly get one child out of her. She had never let him come back again.

And the Lord, the old man said, had preserved the one child he had got out of her from being corrupted by such parents. He had preserved him in the only possible way: the child was dim-witted. The old man would pause here and let the weight of this mystery sink in on Tarwater. He had made, since he learned of that child's existence, several trips into town to try to kidnap him so that he could baptize him, but each time he had come back unsuccessful. The schoolteacher was on his guard and the old man was too fat and stiff now to make an agile kidnapper.

"If by the time I die," he had said to Tarwater, "I haven't got him baptized, it'll be up to you. It'll be the first mission the Lord sends you."

The boy doubted very much that his first mission would be to baptize a dim-witted child. "Oh no it won't be," he said. "He don't mean for me to finish up your leavings. He has other things in mind for me." And he thought of Moses who struck water from a rock, of Joshua who made the sun stand still, of Daniel who stared down lions in the pit.

"It's no part of your job to think for the Lord," his great-uncle said. "Judgment may rack your bones."

The morning the old man died, he came down and cooked the breakfast as usual and died before he got the first spoonful to his mouth. The downstairs of their house was all kitchen, large and dark, with a wood stove at one end of it and a board table drawn up to the stove. Sacks of feed and mash were stacked in the corners and scrapmetal, woodshavings, old rope, ladders, and other tinder were wherever he or Tarwater had let them fall. They had slept in the kitchen until a bobcat sprang in the window one night and frightened his uncle into carrying the bed upstairs where there were two empty rooms. The old man prophesied at the time that the stairsteps would take ten years off his life. At the moment of his death, he sat down to his breakfast and lifted his knife in one square red hand halfway to his mouth, and then with a look of complete astonishment, he lowered it until the hand rested on the edge of the plate and tilted it up off the table.

He was a bull-like old man with a short head set directly into his shoulders and silver protruding eyes that looked like two fish straining to get out of a net of red threads. He had on a putty-colored hat with the brim turned up all around and over his un-

dershirt a grey coat that had once been black. Tarwater, sitting across the table from him, saw red
ropes appear in his face and a tremor pass over him.
It was like the tremor of a quake that had begun at
his heart and run outward and was just reaching the
surface. His mouth twisted down sharply on one side
and he remained exactly as he was, perfectly balanced, his back a good six inches from the chair back
and his stomach caught just under the edge of the
table. His eyes, dead silver, were focussed on the
boy across from him.

Tarwater felt the tremor transfer itself and run
lightly over him. He knew the old man was dead
without touching him and he continued to sit across
the table from the corpse, finishing his breakfast in
a kind of sullen embarrassment as if he were in the
presence of a new personality and couldn't think of
anything to say. Finally he said in a querulous tone,
"Just hold your horses. I already told you I would
do it right." The voice sounded like a stranger's voice,
as if the death had changed him instead of his great-
uncle.

He got up and took his plate out the back door
and set it down on the bottom step and two long-
legged black game roosters tore across the yard and
finished what was on it. He sat down on a long pine
box on the back porch and his hands began absently
to unravel a length of rope while his long face stared
ahead beyond the clearing over the woods that ran
in grey and purple folds until they touched the light

blue fortress line of trees set against the empty morning sky.

Powderhead was not simply off the dirt road but off the wagon track and footpath, and the nearest neighbors, colored not white, still had to walk through the woods, pushing plum branches out of their way to get to it. Once there had been two houses; now there was only the one house with the dead owner inside and the living owner outside on the porch, waiting to bury him. The boy knew he would have to bury the old man before anything would begin. It was as if there would have to be dirt over him before he would be thoroughly dead. The thought seemed to give him respite from something that pressed on him.

A few weeks before, the old man had started an acre of corn to the left and had run it beyond the fenceline almost up to the house on one side. The two strands of barbed-wire ran through the middle of the patch. A line of fog, hump-shaped, was creeping toward it like a white hound dog ready to crouch under and crawl across the yard.

"I'm going to move that fence," Tarwater said. "I ain't going to have any fence I own in the middle of a patch." The voice was loud and strange and disagreeable. Inside his head it continued: you ain't the owner. The schoolteacher owns it.

I own it, Tarwater said, because I'm here and can't nobody get me off. If any schoolteacher comes to claim the property, I'll kill him.

The Lord may send you off, he thought. There was

a complete stillness over everything and the boy felt his heart begin to swell. He held his breath as if he were about to hear a voice from on high. After a few moments he heard a hen scratching beneath him under the porch. He ran his arm fiercely under his nose and gradually his face paled again.

He had on a faded pair of overalls and a grey hat pulled down over his ears like a cap. He followed his uncle's custom of never taking off his hat except in bed. He had always followed his uncle's customs up to this date but: if I want to move that fence before I bury him, it wouldn't be a soul to hinder me, he thought; no voice will be uplifted.

Bury him first and get it over with, the loud stranger's disagreeable voice said. He got up and went to look for the shovel.

The pine box he had been sitting on was his uncle's coffin but he didn't intend to use it. The old man was too heavy for a thin boy to hoist over the side of a box and though old Tarwater had built it himself a few years before, he had said that if it wasn't feasible to get him into it when the time came, then just to put him in the hole as he was, only to be sure the hole was deep. He wanted it ten foot, he said, not just eight. He had worked on the box a long time and when he finished it, he had scratched on the lid, MASON TARWATER, WITH GOD, and had climbed into it where it stood on the back porch, and had lain there for some time, nothing showing but his stomach which rose over the top like over-leavened bread.

The boy had stood at the side of the box, studying him. "This is the end of us all," the old man said with satisfaction, his gravel voice hearty in the coffin.

"It's too much of you for the box," Tarwater said. "I'll have to sit on the lid to press you down or wait until you rot a little."

"Don't wait," old Tarwater had said. "Listen. If it ain't feasible to use the box when the time comes, if you can't lift it or whatever, just get me in the hole but I want it deep. I want it ten foot, not just eight, ten. You can roll me to it if nothing else. I'll roll. Get two boards and set them down the steps and start me rolling and dig where I stop and don't let me roll over into it until it's deep enough. Prop me with some bricks so I won't roll into and don't let the dogs nudge me over the edge before it's finished. You better pen up the dogs," he said.

"What if you die in bed?" the boy asked. "How'm I going to get you down the stairs?"

"I ain't going to die in bed," the old man said. "As soon as I hear the summons, I'm going to run downstairs. I'll get as close to the door as I can. If I should get stuck up there, you'll have to roll me down the stairs, that's all."

"My Lord," the child said.

The old man sat up in the box and brought his fist down on the edge of it. "Listen," he said. "I never asked much of you. I taken you and raised you and saved you from that ass in town and now all I'm asking in return is when I die to get me in the ground where the dead belong and set up a cross over me to show I'm there. That's all in the world I'm asking you to do. I ain't even asking you to go for the niggers and try to get me in the plot with my daddy. I could ask you that but I ain't. I'm doing everything to make it easy for you. All I'm asking you is to get me in the ground and set up a cross."

"I'll be doing good if I get you in the ground," Tarwater said. "I'll be too wore out to set up any cross. I ain't bothering with trifles."

"Trifles!" his uncle hissed. "You'll learn what a trifle is on the day those crosses are gathered! Burying the dead right may be the only honor you ever do yourself. I brought you out here to raise you a Christian, and more than a Christian, a prophet!" he hollered, "and the burden of it will be on you!"

"If I don't have the strength to do it," the child said, watching him with a careful detachment, "I'll notify my uncle in town and he can come out and take care of you. The schoolteacher," he drawled, observing that the pockmarks in his uncle's face had already turned pale against the purple. "He'll tend to you."

The threads that restrained the old man's eyes thickened. He gripped both sides of the coffin and pushed forward as if he were going to drive it off the porch. "He'd burn me," he said hoarsely. "He'd have me cremated in an oven and scatter my ashes. 'Uncle,' he said to me, 'you're a type that's almost extinct!' He'd be willing to pay the undertaker to burn me to be able to scatter my ashes," he said. "He don't believe in the Resurrection. He don't believe in the Last Day. He don't believe in the bread of life . . ."

"The dead don't bother with particulars," the boy interrupted.

The old man grabbed the front of his overalls and pulled him up against the side of the box and glared into his pale face. "The world was made for the dead. Think of all the dead there are," he said, and then as if he had conceived the answer for all the insolence in the world, he said, "There's a million times more dead than living and the dead are dead a million times longer than the living are alive," and he released him with a laugh.

The boy had shown only by a slight quiver that he was shaken by this, and after a minute he had said, "The schoolteacher is my uncle. The only blood connection with good sense I'll have and a living man and if I wanted to go to him, I'd go; now."

The old man looked at him silently for what seemed a full minute. Then he slammed his hands flat on the sides of the box and roared, "Whom the plague beckons, to the plague! Whom the sword to the sword! Whom fire to fire!" And the child trembled visibly.

"I saved you to be free, your own self!" he had shouted, "and not a piece of information inside his head! If you were living with him, you'd be information right now, you'd be inside his head, and what's furthermore," he said, "you'd be going to school."

The boy grimaced. The old man had always impressed on him his good fortune in not being sent to school. The Lord had seen fit to guarantee the purity of his up-bringing, to preserve him from contamination, to preserve him as His elect servant, trained by a prophet for prophesy. While other children his age were herded together in a room to cut out paper pumpkins under the direction of a woman, he was left free for the pursuit of wisdom, the companions of his spirit Abel and Enoch and Noah and Job, Abraham and Moses, King David and Solomon, and all the prophets, from Elijah who escaped death, to John whose severed head struck terror from a dish. The boy knew that escaping school was the surest sign of his election.

The truant officer had come only once. The Lord had told the old man to expect it and what to do and old Tarwater had instructed the boy in his part against the day when, as the devil's emissary, the officer would appear. When the time came and they saw him cutting across the field, they were ready. The child got behind the house and the old man sat on the steps and waited. When the officer, a thin bald-headed man with red galluses, stepped out of the field onto the packed dirt of the yard, he greeted old Tarwater warily and commenced his business as if he had not come for it. He sat down on the steps and spoke of poor weather and poor health. Finally, gazing out over the field, he said, "You got a boy, don't you, that ought to be in school?"

"A fine boy," the old man said, "and I wouldn't stand in his way if anybody thought they could teach him. You boy!" he called. The boy didn't come at once. "Oh you boy!" the old man shouted.

In a few minutes Tarwater appeared from around the side of the house. His eyes were open but not well-focused. His head rolled uncontrollably on his slack shoulders and his tongue lolled in his open mouth.

"He ain't bright," the old man said, "but he's a mighty good boy. He knows to come when you call him."

"Yes," the truant officer said, "well yes, but it might be best to leave him in peace."

"I don't know, he might take to schooling," the old man said. "He ain't had a fit for going on two months."

"I speck he better stay at home," the officer said. "I wouldn't want to put a strain on him," and he commenced to speak of other things. Shortly he took his leave and the two of them watched with satisfaction as the diminishing figure moved back across the field and the red galluses were finally lost to view.

If the schoolteacher had got hold of him, right now he would have been in school, one among many, indistinguishable from the herd, and in the schoolteacher's head, he would be laid out in parts and numbers. "That's where he wanted me," the old man said, "and he thought once he had me in that schoolteacher magazine, I would be as good as in his head." The schoolteacher's house had had little in it but

books and papers. The old man had not known when
he went there to live that every living thing that
passed through the nephew's eyes into his head was
turned by his brain into a book or a paper or a chart.
The schoolteacher had appeared to have a great interest in his being a prophet, chosen by the Lord, and
had asked numerous questions, the answers to which
he had sometimes scratched down on a pad, his little
eyes lighting every now and then as if in some dis-
covery.

The old man had fancied he was making progress
in convincing the nephew again of his Redemption,
for he at least listened though he did not *say* he believed. He seemed to delight to talk about the things
that interested his uncle. He questioned him at length
about his early life, which old Tarwater had practically forgotten. The old man had thought this interest
in his forebears would bear fruit, but what it bore,
what it bore, stench and shame, were dead words.
What it bore was a dry and seedless fruit, incapable
even of rotting, dead from the beginning. From time
to time, the old man would spit out of his mouth, like
gobbets of poison, some of the idiotic sentences from
the schoolteacher's piece. Wrath had burned them on
his memory, word for word. "His fixation of being
called by the Lord had its origin in insecurity. He
needed the assurance of a call, and so he called himself."

"Called myself!" the old man would hiss, "called
myself!" This so enraged him that half the time he

could do nothing but repeat it. "Called myself. I called myself. I, Mason Tarwater, called myself! Called myself to be beaten and tied up. Called myself to be spit on and snickered at. Called myself to be struck down in my pride. Called myself to be torn by the Lord's eye. Listen boy," he would say and grab the child by the straps of his overalls and shake him slowly, "even the mercy of the Lord burns." He would let go the straps and allow the boy to fall back into the thorn bed of that thought, while he continued to hiss and groan.

"Where he wanted me was inside that schoolteacher magazine. He thought once he got me in there, I'd be as good as inside his head and done for and that would be that, that would be the end of it. Well, that wasn't the end of it! Here I sit. And there you sit. In freedom. Not inside anybody's head!" and his voice would run away from him as if it were the freest part of his free self and were straining ahead of his heavy body to be off. Something of his great-uncle's glee would take hold of Tarwater at that point and he would feel that he had escaped some mysterious prison. He even felt he could smell his freedom, pine-scented, coming out of the woods, until the old man would continue, "You were born into bondage and baptized into freedom, into the death of the Lord, into the death of the Lord Jesus Christ."

Then the child would feel a sullenness creeping over him, a slow warm rising resentment that this freedom had to be connected with Jesus and that Jesus had to be the Lord.

"Jesus is the bread of life," the old man said.

The boy, disconcerted, would look off into the distance over the dark blue treeline where the world stretched out, hidden and at its ease. In the darkest, most private part of his soul, hanging upsidedown like a sleeping bat, was the certain, undeniable knowledge that he was not hungry for the bread of life. Had the bush flamed for Moses, the sun stood still for Joshua, the lions turned aside before Daniel only to prophesy the bread of life? Jesus? He felt a terrible disappointment in that conclusion, a dread that it was true. The old man said that as soon as he died, he would hasten to the banks of the Lake of Galilee to eat the loaves and fishes that the Lord had multiplied.

"Forever?" the horrified boy asked.

"Forever," the old man said.

The boy sensed that this was the heart of his greatuncle's madness, this hunger, and what he was secretly afraid of was that it might be passed down, might be hidden in the blood and might strike some day in him and then he would be torn by hunger like the old man, the bottom split out of his stomach so that nothing would heal or fill it but the bread of life.

He tried when possible to pass over these thoughts, to keep his vision located on an even level, to see no more than what was in front of his face and to let his eyes stop at the surface of that. It was as if he were afraid that if he let his eye rest for an instant longer than was needed to place something—a spade, a hoe, the mule's hind quarters before his plow, the red furrow under him—that the thing would suddenly stand before him, strange and terrifying, demanding that he name it and name it justly and be judged for the name he gave it. He did all he could to avoid this threatened intimacy of creation. When the Lord's call came, he wished it to be a voice from out of a clear and empty sky, the trumpet of the Lord God Almighty, untouched by any fleshly hand or breath. He expected to see wheels of fire in the eyes of unearthly beasts. He had expected this to happen as soon as his great-uncle died. He turned his mind off this quickly and went to get the shovel. The schoolteacher is a living man, he thought as he went, but he'd better not come out here and try to get me off this property because I'll kill him. Go to him and be damned, his uncle had said. I've saved you from him this far and if you go to him the minute I'm in the ground there's nothing I can do about it.

The shovel lay against the side of the hen house. "I'll never set my foot in the city again," the boy said to himself aloud. I'll never go to him. Him nor nobody else will ever get me off this place.

He decided to dig the grave under the fig tree because the old man would be good for the figs. The ground was sandy on top and solid brick underneath and the shovel made a clanging sound when he struck it in the sand. Two hundred pounds of dead mountain to bury, he thought, and stood with one foot on the shovel, leaning forward, studying the white sky through the leaves of the tree. It would take all day to get a hole big enough out of this rock and the schoolteacher would burn him in a minute.

Tarwater had seen the schoolteacher once from a distance of about twenty feet and he had seen the dim-witted child closer up. The little boy somewhat resembled old Tarwater except for his eyes which were grey like the old man's but clear, as if the other side of them went down and down into two pools of light. It was plain to look at him that he did not have any sense. The old man had been so shocked by the likeness and the unlikeness that the time he and Tarwater had gone there, he had only stood in the door, staring at the little boy and rolling his tongue around outside his mouth as if he had no sense himself. That had been the first time he had seen the child and he could not forget him. "Married her and got one child out of her and that without sense," he would murmur. "The Lord preserved him and now He means to see he's baptized."

"Well whyn't you get on with it then?" the boy asked, for he wanted something to happen, wanted to see the old man in action, wanted him to kidnap the child and have the schoolteacher have to come after him so that he could get a closer look at his other uncle. "What ails you?" he asked. "What makes you tarry so long? Why don't you make haste and steal him?"

"I take my directions from the Lord God," the old man said, "Who moves in His own time. I don't take them from you."

The white fog had eased through the yard and disappeared into the next bottom and the air was clear and blank. His mind continued to dwell on the schoolteacher's house. "Three months there," his great-uncle had said. "It shames me. Betrayed for three months in the house of my own kin and if when I'm dead you want to turn me over to my betrayer and see my body burned, go ahead! Go ahead, boy," he had shouted, sitting up splotch-faced in his box. "Go ahead and let him burn me but watch out for the Lord's lion after that. Remember the Lord's lion set in the path of the false prophet! I been leavened by the yeast he don't believe in," he had said, "and I won't be burned! And when I'm gone, you'll be better off in these woods by yourself with just as much light as the sun wants to let in than you'll be in the city with him."

He kept on digging but the grave did not get any deeper. "The dead are poor," he said in the voice of the stranger. You can't be any poorer than dead. He'll have to take what he gets. Nobody to bother me, he thought. Ever. No hand uplifted to hinder me from anything; except the Lord's and He ain't said anything. He ain't even noticed me yet.

A sand-colored hound beat its tail on the ground nearby and a few black chickens scratched in the raw clay he was turning up. The sun had slipped over the blue line of trees and circled by a haze of yellow

was moving slowly across the sky. "Now I can do anything I want to," he said, softening the stranger's
voice so that he could stand it. Could kill off all those
chickens if I had a mind to, he thought, watching the
worthless black game bantams that his uncle had
been fond of keeping.

He favored a lot of foolishness, the stranger said.
The truth is he was childish. Why, that schoolteacher
never did him any harm. You take, all he did was to
watch him and write down what he seen and heard
and put it in a paper for schoolteachers to read. Now
what was wrong in that? Why nothing. Who cares
what a schoolteacher reads? And the old fool acted
like he had been killed in his very soul. Well he wasn't
so near dead as he thought he was. Lived on fourteen
years and raised up a boy to bury him, suitable to his
own taste.

As Tarwater slashed at the ground with the shovel,
the stranger's voice took on a kind of restrained fury
and he kept repeating, you got to bury him whole and
completely by hand and that schoolteacher would
burn him in a minute.

After he had dug for an hour or more, the grave
was only a foot deep, not as deep yet as the corpse.
He sat down on the edge of it for a while. The sun
was like a furious white blister in the sky.

The dead are a heap more trouble than the living,
the stranger said. That schoolteacher wouldn't consider for a minute that on the last day all the bodies
marked by crosses will be gathered. In the rest of the

world they do things different than what you been
taught.

"I been there once," Tarwater muttered. "Nobody
has to tell me."

His uncle two or three years before had gone to
call on the lawyers to try to get the property unen-
tailed so that it would skip the schoolteacher and go
to Tarwater. Tarwater had sat at the lawyer's twelfth-
story window and looked down into the pit of the
street while his uncle transacted the business. On the
way from the railroad station he had walked tall in
the mass of moving metal and concrete speckled with
the very small eyes of people. The glitter of his own
eyes was shaded under the stiff roof-like brim of a
new grey hat, balanced perfectly straight on his but-
tressing ears. Before coming he had read facts in the
almanac and he knew that there were 75,000 people
here who were seeing him for the first time. He
wanted to stop and shake hands with each of them
and say his name was F. M. Tarwater and that he
was here only for the day to accompany his uncle on
business at a lawyers. His head jerked backwards
after each passing figure until they began to pass too
thickly and he observed that their eyes didn't grab at
you like the eyes of country people. Several people
bumped into him and this contact that should have
made an acquaintance for life, made nothing because
the hulks shoved on with ducked heads and muttered
apologies that he would have accepted if they had
waited.

Then he had realized, almost without warning, that
this place was evil—the ducked heads, the muttered
words, the hastening away. He saw in a burst of light
that these people were hastening away from the Lord
God Almighty. It was to the city that the prophets
came and he was here in the midst of it. He was here
enjoying what should have repelled him. His lids narrowed with caution and he looked at his uncle who
was rolling on ahead of him, no more concerned with
it all than a bear in the woods. "What kind of prophet
are you?" the boy hissed.

His uncle paid him no attention, did not stop.

"Call yourself a prophet!" he continued in a high
rasping carrying voice.

His uncle stopped and turned. "I'm here on bidnis,"
he said mildly.

"You always said you were a prophet," Tarwater
said. "Now I see what kind of prophet you are. Elijah
would think a heap of you."

His uncle thrust his head forward and his eyes began to bulge. "I'm here on bidnis," he said. "If you
been called by the Lord, then be about your own
mission."

The boy paled slightly and his gaze shifted. "I ain't
been called *yet*," he muttered. "It's you that's been
called."

"And I know what times I'm called and what times
I ain't," his uncle said and turned and paid him no
more attention.

At the lawyer's window, he knelt down and let his

face hang out upsidedown over the floating speckled street moving like a river of tin below and watched the glints on it from the sun which drifted pale in a pale sky, too far away to ignite anything. When he was called, on that day when he returned, he would set the city astir, he would return with fire in his eyes. You have to do something particular here to make them look at you, he thought. They ain't going to look at you just because you're here. He considered his uncle with renewed disgust. When I come for good, he said to himself, I'll do something to make every eye stick on me, and leaning forward, he saw his new hat drop down gently, lost and casual, dallied slightly by the breeze on its way to be smashed in the tin river below. He clutched at his bare head and fell back inside the room.

His uncle was in argument with the lawyer, both hitting the desk that separated them, bending their knees and hitting their fists at the same time. The lawyer, a tall dome-headed man with an eagle's nose, kept repeating in a restrained shriek, "But I didn't make the will. I didn't make the law," and his uncle's gravel voice grated, "I can't help it. My daddy wouldn't have seen a fool inherit his property. That's not how he intended it."

"My hat is gone," Tarwater said.

The lawyer threw himself backwards into his chair and screaked it toward Tarwater and saw him without interest from pale blue eyes and screaked it forward again and said to his uncle, "There's nothing

I can do. You're wasting your time and mine. You might as well resign yourself to this will."

"Listen," old Tarwater said, "at one time I thought I was finished, old and sick and about to die and no money, nothing, and I accepted his hospitality because he was my closest blood connection and you could have called it his duty to take me, only I thought it was Charity, I thought . . ."

"I can't help what you thought or did or what your connection thought or did," the lawyer said and closed his eyes.

"My hat fell," Tarwater said.

"I'm only a lawyer," the lawyer said, letting his glance rove over the lines of clay-colored books of law that fortressed his office.

"A car is liable to have run over it by now."

"Listen," his uncle said, "all the time he was studying me for this paper. Taking secret tests on me, his own kin, crawling into my soul through the back door and then says to me, 'Uncle, you're a type that's almost extinct!' Almost extinct!" the old man piped, barely able to force a thread of sound from his throat. "You see how extinct I am!"

The lawyer closed his eyes again and smiled into one cheek.

"Other lawyers," the old man growled and they had left and visited three more, without stopping, and Tarwater had counted eleven men who might have had on his hat or might not. Finally when they came out of the fourth lawyer's office, they sat down

on the window ledge of a bank building and his uncle
felt in his pocket for some biscuits he had brought
and handed one to Tarwater. The old man unbut-
toned his coat and allowed his stomach to ease forward and rest on his lap while he ate. His face
worked wrathfully; the skin between the pockmarks
appeared to jump from one spot to another. Tarwater
was very pale and his eyes glittered with a peculiar
hollow depth. He had an old work kerchief tied
around his head, knotted at the four corners. He
didn't observe the passing people who observed him
now. "Thank God we're finished and can go home,"
he muttered.

"We ain't finished here," the old man said and got
up abruptly and started down the street.

"My Lord!" the boy groaned, jumping to catch up
with him. "Can't we sit down for one minute? Ain't
you got any sense? They all tell you the same thing.
It's only one law and it's nothing you can do about
it. I got sense enough to get that; why ain't you?
What's the matter with you?"

The old man strode on with his head thrust forward as if he were smelling out an enemy.

"Where we going?" Tarwater asked after they had
walked out of the business streets and were passing
between rows of grey bulbous houses with sooty
porches that overhung the sidewalks. "Listen," he
said, hitting at his uncle's hip, "I never ast to come."

"You would have ast to come soon enough," the old
man muttered. "Get your fill now."

"I never ast for no fill. I never ast to come at all. I'm here before I knew this here was here."

"Just remember," the old man said, "just remember that I told you to remember when you ast to come that you never liked it when you were here," and they kept on going, crossing one length of sidewalk after another, row after row of overhanging houses with half-open doors that let a little dried light fall on the stained passageways inside. Finally they came out into another section where the houses were clean and squat and almost identical and each had a square of grass in front of it. After a few blocks Tarwater dropped down on the sidewalk and said, "I ain't going no further. I don't even know where I'm going and I ain't going no further." His uncle didn't stop or look back. In a second he jumped up and followed him again in a panic lest he be left.

The old man kept straining forward as if his blood scent were leading him closer and closer to the place where his enemy was hiding. He suddenly turned up the short walk of a pale yellow brick house and moved rigidly to the white door, his heavy shoulders hunched as if he were going to crash through it. He struck the wood with his fist, ignoring a polished brass knocker. At that instant Tarwater realized that this was where the schoolteacher lived, and he stopped where he was and remained rigid, his eye on the door. He knew by some obscure instinct that the door was going to open and reveal his destiny. In his mind's eye, he saw the schoolteacher about to appear in it, lean and evil, waiting to engage whom the Lord would send to conquer him. The boy clamped his teeth together to keep them from chattering. The door opened.

A small pink-faced boy stood in it with his mouth hung in a silly smile. He had white hair and a knobby forehead. He wore steel-rimmed spectacles and had pale silver eyes like the old man's except that they were clear and empty. He was gnawing on a brown apple core.

The old man stared at him, his lips parting slowly until his mouth hung open. He looked as if he beheld an unspeakable mystery. The little boy made an unintelligible noise and pushed the door almost shut, hiding himself all but one spectacled eye.

Suddenly a tremendous indignation seized Tarwater. He eyed the small face peering from the crack. He searched his mind fiercely for the right word to hurl at it. Finally he said in a slow emphatic voice, "Before you was here, *I* was here."

The old man caught his shoulder and pulled him back. "He don't have good sense," he said. "Can't you see he don't have good sense? He don't know what you're talking about."

The boy grew more furious than ever. He swung around on his heel to leave.

"Wait," his uncle said and caught him. "Get behind that hedge yonder and hide yourself. I'm going in there and baptize him."

Tarwater's mouth was agape.

"Get behind there like I told you," he said and gave him a push toward the hedge. Then the old man braced himself. He turned and went back to the door. Just as he reached it, it was flung open and a lean young man with heavy black-rimmed spectacles stood in it, his head thrust forward, glaring at him.

Old Tarwater raised his fist. "The Lord Jesus Christ sent me to baptize that boy!" he shouted. "Stand aside. I mean to do it!"

Tarwater's head popped up from behind the hedge. Breathlessly he took the schoolteacher in—the narrow boney face slanting backwards from the jutting jaw, the hair that receded from the high forehead, the eyes encircled in glass. The white-haired child had caught hold of his father's leg and was hanging onto it. The schoolteacher pushed him back inside the house. Then he stepped outside and slammed the door behind him and continued to glare at the old man as if he dared him to take a step.

"That boy cries out for his baptism," the old man said. "Precious in the sight of the Lord even an idiot!"

"Get off my property," the nephew said in a tight voice as if he were keeping it calm by force. "If you don't, I'll have you put back in the asylum where you belong."

"You can't touch the servant of the Lord!" the old man hollered.

"You get away from here!" the nephew shouted, losing control of his voice. "Ask the Lord why He made him an idiot in the first place, uncle. Tell him I want to know why!"

The boy's heart was beating so fast he was afraid it was going to gallop out of his chest and disappear forever. He was head and shoulders out of the shrubbery.

"Yours not to ask!" the old man shouted. "Yours not to question the mind of the Lord God Almighty. Yours not to grind the Lord into your head and spit out a number!"

"Where's the boy?" the nephew asked, looking around suddenly as if he had just thought of it. "Where's the boy you were going to raise into a prophet to burn my eyes clean?" and he laughed.

Tarwater lowered his head into the bush again, instantly disliking the schoolteacher's laugh which seemed to reduce him to the least importance.

"His day is going to come," the old man said. "Either him or me is going to baptize that child. If not me in my day, him in his."

"You'll never lay a hand on him," the schoolteacher said. "You could slosh water on him for the rest of his life and he'd still be an idiot. Five years old for all eternity, useless forever. Listen," he said, and the boy heard his taut voice turn low with a kind of subdued intensity, a passion equal and opposite to the old man's, "he'll never be baptized—just as a matter of principle, nothing else. As a gesture of human dignity, he'll never be baptized."

"Time will discover the hand that baptizes him," the old man said.

"Time will discover it," the nephew said and opened the door behind him and stepped back inside and slammed it on himself.

The boy had risen from the shrubbery, his head swirling with excitement. He had never been back there again, never seen his cousin again, never seen the schoolteacher again, and he hoped to God, he told the stranger digging the grave along with him now that he would never see him again though he had nothing against him himself and he would dislike to have to kill him but if he came out here, messing in what was none of his business except by law, then he would be obliged to.

Listen, the stranger said, what would he want to come out here for—where there's nothing?

Tarwater didn't answer. He didn't search out the stranger's face but he knew by now that it was sharp and friendly and wise, shadowed under a stiff broad-brimmed panama hat that obscured the color of his eyes. He had lost his dislike for the thought of the voice. Only every now and then it sounded like a stranger's voice to him. He began to feel that he was only just now meeting himself, as if as long as his uncle had lived, he had been deprived of his own acquaintance. I ain't denying the old man was a good one, his new friend said, but like you said: you can't be any poorer than dead. They have to take what they can get. His soul is off this mortal earth now and his body is not going to feel the pinch, of fire or anything else.

"It was the last day he was thinking of," Tarwater murmured.

Well now, the stranger said, don't you think any cross you set up in the year 1952 would be rotted out by the year the Day of Judgment comes in? Rotted to as much dust as his ashes if you reduced him to ashes? And lemme ast you this: what's God going to do with sailors drowned at sea that the fish have et and the fish that et them et by other fish and they et by yet others? And what about people that get burned up naturally in house fires? Burnt up one way or another or lost in machines until they're pulp? And all those sojers blasted to nothing? What about all those that there's nothing left of to burn or bury?

If I burnt him, Tarwater said, it wouldn't be natural, it would be deliberate.

Oh I see, the stranger said. It ain't the Day of Judgment for him you're worried about. It's the Day of Judgment for you.

That's my bidnis, Tarwater said.

I ain't buttin into your bidnis, the stranger said. It don't mean a thing to me. You're left by yourself in this empty place. Forever by yourself in this empty place with just as much light as that dwarf sun wants to let in. You don't mean a thing to a soul as far as I can see.

"Redeemed," Tarwater muttered.

Do you smoke? the stranger asked.

Smoke if I want to and don't if I don't, Tarwater said. Bury if need be and don't if don't.

Go take a look at him and see if he's fell off his chair, his friend suggested.

Tarwater let the shovel drop in the grave and returned to the house. He opened the front door a crack and put his face to it. His uncle glared slightly to the side of him like a judge intent upon some terrible evidence. The boy shut the door quickly and went back to the grave, cold in spite of the sweat that stuck his shirt to his back. He began digging again.

The schoolteacher was too smart for him, that's all, the stranger said presently. You remember well enough how he said he kidnapped him when the schoolteacher was seven years of age. Gone to town and persuaded him out of his own backyard and brought him out here and baptized him. And what come of it? Nothing. The schoolteacher don't care now if he's baptized or if he ain't. It don't mean a thing to him one way or the other. Don't care if he's Redeemed or not neither. He only spent four days out here; you've spent fourteen years and now got to spend the rest of your life.

You see he was crazy all along, he continued. Wanted to make a prophet out of that schoolteacher too, but the schoolteacher was too smart for him. He got away.

He had somebody to come for him, Tarwater said. His daddy came and got him back. Nobody came and got me back.

The schoolteacher himself come after you, the stranger said, and got shot in the leg and the ear for his trouble.

I was not yet one year old, Tarwater said. A baby can't walk off and leave.

You ain't a baby now, his friend said.

The grave did not appear to get any deeper though he continued to dig. Look at the big prophet, the stranger jeered, and watched him from the shade of the speckled tree shadows. Lemme hear you prophesy something. The truth is the Lord ain't studying about you. You ain't entered His Head.

Tarwater turned around abruptly and worked from the other side and the voice continued from behind him. Anybody that's a prophet has got to have somebody to prophesy to. Unless you're just going to prophesy to yourself, he amended—or go baptize that dim-witted child, he added in a tone of high sarcasm.

The truth is, he said after a minute, the truth is that you're just as smart, if you ain't actually smarter, than the schoolteacher. Because he had somebody—his daddy and his mother—to tell him the old man was crazy, whereas you ain't had anybody and yet you've figured it out for yourself. Of course, it's taken you longer, but you've come to the right conclusion: you know he was a crazy man even when he wasn't in the asylum, even those last years.

Or if he wasn't actually crazy, he was the same thing in a different way: he didn't have but one thing on his mind. He was a one-notion man. Jesus. Jesus this and Jesus that. Ain't you in all your fourteen years of supporting his foolishness fed up and sick to the roof of your mouth with Jesus? My Lord and Saviour, the stranger sighed, I am if you ain't.

After a pause he continued. The way I see it, he said, you can do one of two things. One of them, not both. Nobody can do both of two things without straining themselves. You can do one thing or you can do the opposite.

Jesus or the devil, the boy said.

No no no, the stranger said, there ain't no such thing as a devil. I can tell you that from my own self-experience. I know that for a fact. It ain't Jesus or the devil. It's Jesus or *you.*

Jesus or me, Tarwater repeated. He put the shovel down for a rest and thought: he said the schoolteacher was glad to come. He said all he had to do was go out in the schoolteacher's back yard where he was playing and say, Let's you and me go to the country for a while—you have to be born again. The Lord Jesus Christ sent me to see to it. And the schoolteacher got up and took hold of his hand without a word and came with him and all the four days while he was out here he said the schoolteacher was hoping they wouldn't come for him.

Well that's all the sense a seven-year-old boy's got, the stranger said. You can't expect no more from a child. He learned better as soon as he got back to town; his daddy told him the old man was crazy and not to believe a word of what all he had learnt him.

That's not the way he told it, Tarwater said. He said that when the schoolteacher was seven years old, he had good sense but later it dried up. His daddy was an ass and not fit to raise him and his mother was a whore. She ran away from here when she was eighteen years old.

It took her that long? the stranger said in an incredulous tone. My, she was kind of a ass herself.

My great uncle said he hated to admit it that his own sister was a whore but he had to say it to say the truth, the boy said.

Shaw, you know yourself that it give him great satisfaction to admit she was a whore, the stranger said. He was always admitting somebody was an ass or a whore. That's all a prophet is good for—to admit somebody else is an ass or a whore. And anyway, he asked slyly, what do you know about whores? Where have you ever run up on one of them?

Certainly I know what one of them is, the boy said.

The Bible was full of them. He knew what they were and to what they were liable to come, and just as Jezebel was discovered by dogs, an arm here and a foot there, so said his great-uncle, it had almost been with his own mother and grandmother. The two of them, along with his grandfather, had been killed in an automobile crash, leaving only the schoolteacher alive in that family, and Tarwater himself, for his mother (unmarried and shameless) had lived just long enough after the crash for him to be born. He had been born at the scene of the wreck.

The boy was very proud that he had been born in a wreck. He had always felt that it set his existence apart from the ordinary one and he had understood from it that the plans of God for him were special, even though nothing of consequence had happened to him so far. Often when he walked in the woods and came upon some bush a little removed from the rest, his breath would catch in his throat and he would stop and wait for the bush to burst into flame. It had not done it yet.

His uncle had never seemed to be aware of the importance of the way he had been born, only of how he had been born again. He would often ask him why he thought the Lord had rescued him out of the womb of a whore and let him see the light of day at all, and then why, having done it once, He had gone and done it again, allowing him to be baptized by his great-uncle into the death of Christ, and then having done it twice, gone on and done it a third time, allowing him to be rescued by his great-uncle from the schoolteacher and brought to the backwoods and given a chance to be brought up according to the truth. It was because, his uncle said, the Lord meant him to be trained for a prophet, even though he was a bastard, and to take his great-uncle's place when he died. The old man compared their situation to that of Elijah and Elisha.

All right, the stranger said, I suppose you know what one of them is. But there's a heap else you don't know. You go ahead and put your feet in his shoes. Elisha after Elijah like he said. But just lemme ast you this: where is the voice of the Lord? I haven't heard it. Who's called you this morning? Or any morning? Have you been told what to do? You ain't even heard the sound of natural thunder this morning. There ain't a cloud in the sky. The trouble with you, I see, he concluded, is that you ain't got but just enough sense to believe every word he told you.

The sun was directly overhead, apparently dead still, holding its breath, waiting out the noontime. The grave was about two feet deep. Ten foot now, remember, the stranger said and laughed. Old men are selfish. You got to expect the least of them. The least of everybody, he added and let out a flat sigh that was like a gust of sand raised and dropped suddenly by the wind.

Tarwater looked up and saw two figures cutting across the field, a colored man and woman, each dangling an empty vinegar jug by a finger. The woman, tall and Indianlike, had on a green sun hat. She stooped under the fence without pausing and came on across the yard toward the grave; the man held the wire down and swung his leg over and followed at her elbow. They kept their eyes on the hole and stopped at the edge of it, looking down into the raw ground with shocked satisfied expressions. The man,

Buford, had a crinkled face, darker than his hat. "Old man passed," he said.

The woman lifted her head and let out a slow sustained wail, piercing and formal. She set her jug down on the ground and crossed her arms and then lifted them in the air and wailed again.

"Tell her to shut up that," Tarwater said. "I'm in charge here now and I don't want no nigger-mourning."

"I seen his spirit for two nights," she said. "Seen him two nights and he was unrested."

"He ain't been dead but since this morning," Tarwater said. "If you all want your jugs filled, give them to me and dig while I'm gone."

"He'd been predicting his passing for many years," Buford said. "She seen him in her dream several nights and he wasn't rested. I known him well. I known him very well indeed."

"Poor sweet sugar boy," the woman said to Tarwater, "what you going to do here now by yourself in this lonesome place?"

"Mind my bidnis," the boy said, jerking the jug out of her hand. He started off so quickly that he almost fell. He stalked across the back field toward the rim of trees that surrounded the clearing.

The birds had gone into the deep woods to escape the noon sun and one thrush, hidden some distance ahead of him, called the same four notes again and again, stopping each time after them to make a silence. Tarwater began to walk faster, then he began to lope, and in a second he was running like something hunted, sliding down slopes waxed with pine needles and grasping the limbs of trees to pull himself, panting, up the slippery inclines. He crashed through a wall of honeysuckle and lept across a sandy near-dry stream bed and fell down against the high clay bank that formed the back wall of a cove where the old man kept his extra liquor hidden. He hid it in a hollow of the bank, covered with a large stone. Tarwater began to fight at the stone to pull it away, while the stranger stood over his shoulder panting, he was crazy! He was crazy! That's the long and short of it, he was crazy!

Tarwater got the stone away and pulled out a black jug and sat down against the bank with it. Crazy! the stranger hissed, collapsing by his side.

The sun appeared, a furious white, edging its way secretly behind the tops of the trees that rose over the hiding place.

A man, seventy years of age, to bring a baby out into the backwoods to raise him right! Suppose he had died when you were four years old instead of fourteen? Could you have toted mash to the still then and supported yourself? I never heard of no four-year-old running a still.

Never did I hear of that, he continued. You weren't anything to him but something that would grow big enough to bury him when the time came and now that he's dead, he's shut of you but you got two hun-

dred and fifty pounds of him to put below the face of
the earth. And don't think he wouldn't heat up like a
coal stove to see you take a drop of liquor, he added.
Though he had a weakness for it himself. When he
couldn't stand the Lord one instant longer, he got
drunk, prophet or no prophet. Hah. He might say it
would hurt you but what he meant was you might get
so much you wouldn't be in no fit condition to bury
him. He said he brought you out here to raise you according to principle and that was the principle: that
you should be fit when the time came to bury him so
he would have a cross to mark where he was at.

A prophet with a still! He's the only prophet I ever
heard of making liquor for a living.

After a minute he said in a softer tone as the boy
took a long swallow from the black jug, well, a little
won't interfere. Moderation never hurt no one.

A burning arm slid down Tarwater's throat as if
the devil were already reaching inside him to finger
his soul. He squinted at the angry sun creeping behind the topmost fringe of trees.

Take it easy, his friend said. Do you remember
them nigger gospel singers you saw one time, all
drunk, all singing, all dancing around that black Ford
automobile? Jesus, they wouldn't have been near so
glad they were Redeemed if they hadn't had that
liquor in them. I wouldn't pay too much attention to
my Redemption if I was you. Some people take everything too hard.

Tarwater drank more slowly. He had been drunk

only one time before and that time his uncle had beat him with a piece of crate for it, saying liquor would dissolve a child's gut, another of his lies because his gut had not dissolved.

It should be clear to you, his kind friend said, how all your life you been tricked by that old man. You could have been a city slicker for the last fourteen years. Instead, you been deprived of any company but his, you been living in a two-story barn in the middle of this earth's bald patch, following behind a mule and plow since you were seven. And how do you know the education he give you is true to the facts? Maybe he taught you a system of figures nobody else uses? How do you know that two added to two makes four? Four added to four makes eight? Maybe other people don't think so. How do you know if there was an Adam or if Jesus eased your situation any when He redeemed you? Or how do you know if He actually done it? Nothing but that old man's word and it ought to be obvious to you by now that he was crazy. And as for Judgment Day, the stranger said, every day is Judgment Day.

Ain't you old enough to have learnt that yet for yourself? Don't everything you do, everything you have ever done, work itself out right or wrong before your eye and usually before the sun has set? Have you ever got by with anything? No you ain't nor ever thought you would. You might as well drink all that liquor since you've already drunk so much. Once you pass the moderation mark you've passed it, and that gyration you feel working down from the top of your brain, he said, that's the Hand of God laying a blessing on you. He has given you your release. That old man was the stone before your door and the Lord has rolled it away. He ain't rolled it quite far enough, of course. You got to finish up yourself but He's done the main part. Praise Him.

Tarwater had ceased to have any feeling in his legs. He dozed for a while, his head hanging to the side and his mouth open and the liquor trickling slowly down the side of his overalls where the jug had overturned in his lap. Eventually there was only a drip at the neck of the bottle, forming and filling and dropping, silent and measured and sun-colored. The bright even sky began to fade, coarsening with clouds until every shadow had gone in. He woke with a wrench forward, his eyes focussing and unfocussing on something that looked like a burnt rag hanging close to his face.

Buford said, "This ain't no way for you to act. Old man don't deserve this. There's no rest until the dead is buried." He was squatting on his heels, one hand gripped around Tarwater's arm. "I gone yonder to the door and seen him sitting there at the table, not even laid out on a cooling board. He ought to be laid out and have some salt on his bosom if you mean to keep him overnight."

The boy's lids pinched together to hold the image steady and in a second he made out two small red blistered eyes.

"He deserves to lie in a grave that fits him," Buford said. "He was deep in this life, he was deep in Jesus' misery."

"Nigger," the child said, working his strange swollen tongue, "take your hand off me."

Buford lifted his hand. "He needs to be rested," he said.

"He'll be rested all right when I get through with him," Tarwater said vaguely. "Go on and lea' me to my bidnis."

"Nobody going to bother you," Buford said, standing up. He waited a minute, bent, looking down at the limp figure sprawled against the bank. The boy's head was tilted backwards over a root that jutted out of the clay wall. His mouth hung open and his turned-up hat cut a straight line across his forehead, just over his half-open unseeing eyes. His cheekbones protruded, narrow and thin like the arms of a cross, and the hollows under them had an ancient look as if the child's skeleton beneath were as old as the world. "Nobody going to bother you," the Negro muttered, pushing through the wall of honeysuckle without looking back. "That going to be your trouble."

Tarwater closed his eyes again.

Some night bird complaining close by woke him up. It was not a screeching noise, only an intermittent hump-hump as if the bird had to recall his grievance each time before he repeated it. Clouds were moving convulsively across a black sky and there was

a pink unsteady moon that appeared to be jerked up
a foot or so and then dropped and jerked up again.
This was because, as he observed in an instant, the
sky was lowering, coming down fast to smother him.
The bird screeched and flew off in time and Tarwater
lurched into the middle of the stream bed and
crouched on his hands and knees. The moon was reflected like pale fire in the few spots of water in the
sand. He sprang at the wall of honeysuckle and began
to tear through it, confusing the sweet familiar odor
with the weight coming down on him. When he stood
up on the other side, the black ground swung slowly
and threw him down again. A flare of pink lightning
lit the woods and he saw the black shapes of trees
pierce out of the ground all around him. The night
bird began to hump again from a thicket where he
had settled.

He got up and began to move in the direction of
the clearing, feeling his way from tree to tree, the
trunks very cold and dry to his touch. There was distant thunder and a continuous flicker of pale lightning firing one section of woods and then another.
Finally he saw the shack, standing gaunt-black and
tall in the middle of the clearing, with the pink moon
trembling directly over it. His eyes glittered like open
pits of light as he moved across the sand, dragging
his crushed shadow behind him. He didn't turn his
head to that side of the yard where he had started the
grave. He stopped at the far back corner of the house
and squatted down on the ground and looked under-

neath at the litter there, chicken crates and barrels and old rags and boxes. He had a small box of wooden matches in his pocket.

He crawled under and began to set small fires, building one from another, and working his way out at the front porch, leaving the fire behind him eating greedily at the dry tinder and the floor boards of the house. He crossed the front side of the yard and went through the rutted field without looking back until he reached the edge of the opposite woods. Then he glanced over his shoulder and saw that the pink moon had dropped through the roof of the shack and was bursting and he began to run, forced on through the woods by two bulging silver eyes that grew in immense astonishment in the center of the fire behind him. He could hear it moving up through the black night like a whirling chariot.

Toward midnight he came out on the highway and caught a ride with a salesman who was a manufacturer's representative, selling copper flues throughout the Southeast, and who gave the silent boy what he said was the best advice he could give any young fellow setting out to find himself a place in the world. While they sped forward on the black untwisting highway, watched on either side by a dark wall of trees, the salesman said that it had been his personal experience that you couldn't sell a copper flue to a man you didn't love. He was a thin fellow with a narrow face that appeared to have been worn down to the sharpest possible depressions. He wore a broad-brimmed stiff grey hat of the kind used by business-men who would like to look like cowboys. He said love was the only policy that worked 95% of the time. He said when he went to sell a man a flue, he asked first about that man's wife's health and how his children were. He said he had a book that he kept the names of his customer's families in and what was wrong with them. A man's wife had cancer, he put her name down in the book and wrote *cancer* after it and inquired about her every time he went to that man's hardware store until she died; then he scratched out the word *cancer* and wrote *dead* there. "And I say thank God when they're dead," the salesman said; "that's one less to remember."

"You don't owe the dead anything," Tarwater said in a loud voice, speaking for almost the first time since he had got in the car.

"Nor they you," said the stranger. "And that's the way it ought to be in this world—nobody owing nobody nothing."

"Look," Tarwater said suddenly, sitting forward, his face close to the windshield, "we're headed in the wrong direction. We're going back where we came from. There's the fire again. There's the fire we left!"

Ahead of them in the sky there was a faint glow, steady, and not made by lightning. "That's the same fire we came from!" the boy said in a high voice.

"Boy, you must be nuts," the salesman said. "That's the city we're coming to. That's the glow from the city lights. I reckon this is your first trip anywhere."

"You're turned around," the child said; "it's the same fire."

The stranger twisted his rutted face sharply. "I've never been turned around in my life," he said. "And I didn't come from any fire. I come from Mobile. And I know where I'm going. What's the matter with you?"

Tarwater sat staring at the glow in front of him. "I was asleep," he muttered. "I'm just now waking up."

"You should have been listening to me," the salesman said. "I been telling you things you ought to know."

II

IF THE boy had actually trusted his new friend, Meeks, the copper flue salesman, he would have accepted Meeks' offer to take him directly to his uncle's door and let him out. Meeks had turned on the car light and told him to climb over onto the back seat and root around until he found the telephone book and when Tarwater had climbed back with it, he had showed him how to find his uncle's name in the book. Tarwater wrote the address and the telephone number down on the back of one of Meeks' cards. Meeks' telephone number was on the other side and he said any time Tarwater wanted to contact him for a little loan or any assistance, not to be afraid to use it. What Meeks had decided after about a half hour of the boy was that he was just enough off in the head and just ignorant enough to be a very hard worker, and he wanted a very ignorant energetic boy to work for him. But Tarwater was evasive. "I got to contact this uncle of mine, my only blood connection," he said.

Meeks could look at this boy and tell that he was running away from home, that he had left a mother and probably a sot-father and probably four or five brothers and sisters in a two-room shack set in a brush-swept bare-ground clearing just off the high-way and that he was hightailing it for the big world, having first, from the way he reeked, fortified himself with stump liquor. He didn't for a minute believe he had any uncle at any such respectable address. He thought the boy had set his finger down on the name, Rayber, by chance and said, "That's him. A school-teacher. My uncle."

"I'll take you right to his door," Meeks had said, fox-like. "We pass there going through town. We pass right by there."

"No," Tarwater said. He was sitting forward on the seat, looking out the window at a hill covered with old used-car bodies. In the indistinct darkness, they seemed to be drowning into the ground, to be about half-submerged already. The city hung in front of them on the side of the mountain as if it were a larger part of the same pile, not yet buried so deep. The fire

had gone out of it and it appeared settled into its un-
breakable parts.

The boy did not intend to go to the schoolteacher's
until daylight and when he went he intended to make
it plain that he had not come to be beholden or to be
studied for a schoolteacher magazine. He began trying to remember the schoolteacher's face so that he
could stare him down in his mind before he actually
faced him. He felt that the more he could recall about
him, the less advantage the new uncle would have
over him. The face had not been one that held together in his mind, though he remembered the slop-
ing jaw and the black-rimmed glasses. What he could
not picture were the eyes behind the glasses. He had
no memory of them and there was every kind of con-
tradiction in the rubble of his great-uncle's descrip-
tions. Sometimes the old man had said the nephew's
eyes were black and sometimes brown. The boy kept
trying to find eyes that fit mouth, nose that fit chin,
but every time he thought he had a face put together,
it fell apart and he had to begin on a new one. It was
as if the schoolteacher, like the devil, could take on
any look that suited him.

Meeks was telling him about the value of work. He
said that it had been his personal experience that if
you wanted to get ahead, you had to work. He said
this was the law of life and it was no way to get
around it because it was inscribed on the human
heart like love thy neighbor. He said these two laws

were the team that worked together to make the world go round and that any individual who wanted to be a success and win the pursuit of happiness, that was all he needed to know.

The boy was beginning to see a consistent image for the schoolteacher's eyes and was not listening to this advice. He saw them dark grey, shadowed with knowledge, and the knowledge moved like tree reflections in a pond where far below the surface shadows a snake may glide and disappear. He had made a habit of catching his great-uncle in contradictions about the schoolteacher's appearance.

"I forget what color eyes he's got," the old man would say, irked. "What difference does the color make when I know the look? I know what's behind it."

"What's behind it?"

"Nothing. He's full of nothing."

"He knows a heap," the boy said. "I don't reckon it's anything he don't know."

"He don't know it's anything he can't know," the old man said. "That's his trouble. He thinks if it's something he can't know then somebody smarter than him can tell him about it and he can know it just the same. And if you were to go there, the first thing he would do would be to test your head and tell you what you were thinking and howcome you were thinking it and what you ought to be thinking instead. And before long you wouldn't belong to your self no more, you would belong to him."

The boy had no intention of allowing this to happen. He knew enough about the schoolteacher to be on his guard. He knew two complete histories, the history of the world, beginning with Adam, and the history of the schoolteacher, beginning with his mother, old Tarwater's own and only sister who had run away from Powderhead when she was eighteen years old and had become—the old man said he would mince no words, even with a child—a whore, until she had found a man by the name of Rayber who was willing to marry one. At least once a week, beginning at the beginning, the old man had reviewed this history through to the end.

His sister and this Rayber had brought two children into the world, one the schoolteacher and one a girl who had turned out to be Tarwater's mother and who, the old man said, had followed in the natural footsteps of her own mother, being already a whore by the time she was eighteen.

The old man had a great deal to say about Tarwater's conception, for the schoolteacher had told him that he himself had got his sister this first (and last) lover because he thought it would contribute to her *self-confidence*. The old man would say this, imitating the schoolteacher's voice and making it sillier than the boy felt it probably was. The old man was thrown into a fury of exasperation that there was not enough scorn in the world to cast upon this idiocy. Finally he would give up trying. The lover had shot himself after the accident, which was a relief to the schoolteacher for he wanted to bring up the baby himself.

The old man said that with the devil having such a heavy role in his beginning, it was little wonder that he should have an eye on the boy and keep him under close surveillance during his time on earth, in order that the soul he had helped call into being might serve him forever in hell. "You are the kind of boy," the old man said, "that the devil is always going to be offering to assist, to give you a smoke or a drink or a ride, and to ask you your bidnis. You had better mind how you take up with strangers. And keep your bidnis to yourself." It was to foil the devil's plans for him that the Lord had seen to his upbringing.

"What line you going to get into?" Meeks asked.

The boy didn't appear to hear.

Whereas the schoolteacher had led his sister into evil, with success, old Tarwater had made every attempt to lead his own sister to repentance, without success. Through one means or another, he had managed to keep up with her after she ran away from Powderhead; but even after she married, she would not listen to any word that had to do with her salvation. He had twice been thrown out of her house by her husband—each time with the assistance of the police because the husband was a man of no force—but the Lord had prompted him constantly to go back, even in the face of going to jail. When he could not get inside the house, he would stand outside it and shout and then she would let him in lest he at-

tract the attention of the neighbors. The neighborhood children would gather to listen to him and she
would have to let him in.

It was not to be wondered at, the old man would
say, that the schoolteacher was no better than he was
with such a father as he had. The man, an insurance
salesman, wore a straw hat on the side of his head
and smoked a cigar and when you told him his soul
was in danger, he offered to sell you a policy against
any contingency. He said he was a prophet too, a
prophet of life insurance, for every right-thinking
Christian, he said, knew that it was his Christian duty
to protect his family and provide for them in the
event of the unexpected. There was no use treating
with him, the old man said; his brain was as slick as
his eyeballs and the truth would no more soak into it
than rain would penetrate tin. The schoolteacher,
with Tarwater blood in him, at least had his father's
strain diluted. "Good blood flows in his veins," the old
man said. "And good blood knows the Lord and there
ain't a thing he can do about having it. There ain't a
way in the world he can get rid of it."

Meeks abruptly poked the boy in the side with his
elbow. He said if it was one thing a person needed to
learn it was to pay attention to older people than him
when they gave him good advice. He said he himself
had graduated from the School of Experience with
an H.L.L. degree. He asked the boy if he knew what
was an H.L.L. degree. Tarwater shook his head.
Meeks said the H.L.L. degree was the Hard Lesson

from Life degree. He said it was the quickest got and that it stayed learnt the longest.

The boy turned his head to the window.

One day the old man's sister had worked a perfidy on him. He had been in the habit of going on Wednesday afternoon because on that afternoon the husband played a golf game and he could find her alone. On this particular Wednesday, she did not open the door but he knew she was inside because he heard footsteps. He beat on the door a few times to warn her and when she wouldn't open it, he began to shout, for her and for all who would hear.

While he was telling this to Tarwater, he would jump up and begin to shout and prophesy there in the clearing the same way he had done it in front of her door. With no one to hear but the boy, he would flail his arms and roar, "Ignore the Lord Jesus as long as you can! Spit out the bread of life and sicken on honey. Whom work beckons, to work! Whom blood to blood! Whom lust to lust! Make haste, make haste. Fly faster and faster. Spin yourselves in a frenzy, the time is short! The Lord is preparing a prophet. The Lord is preparing a prophet with fire in his hand and eye and the prophet is moving toward the city with his warning. The prophet is coming with the Lord's message. 'Go warn the children of God,' saith the Lord, 'of the terrible speed of justice.' Who will be left? Who will be left when the Lord's mercy strikes?"

He might have been shouting to the silent woods that encircled them. While he was in his frenzy, the boy would take up the shotgun and hold it to his eye and sight along the barrel, but sometimes as his uncle grew more and more wild, he would lift his face from the gun for a moment with a look of uneasy alertness, as if while he had been inattentive, the old man's words had been dropping one by one into him and now, silent, hidden in his bloodstream, were moving secretly toward some goal of their own.

His uncle would prophesy until he exhausted himself and then he would fall with a thud on the swayback step and sometimes it would be five or ten minutes before he could go on and relate how the sister had worked the perfidy on him.

Whenever he came to this part of the story, his breath would at once come short as if he were struggling to run up a hill. His face would get redder and his voice thinner and sometimes it would give out completely and he would sit there on the step, beating the porch floor with his fist while he moved his lips and no sound came out. Finally he would pipe, "They grabbed me. Two. From behind. The door behind. Two."

His sister had had two men and a doctor behind the door, listening, and the papers made out to commit him to the asylum if the doctor thought he was crazy. When he understood what was happening, he had raged through her house like a blinded bull, everything crashing behind him, and it had taken two of them and the doctor and two neighbors to get him down. The doctor had said he was not only crazy but dangerous and they had taken him to the asylum in a strait jacket.

"Ezekiel was in the pit for forty days," he would say, "but I was in it for four years," and he would stop at that point and warn Tarwater that the servants of the Lord Jesus could expect the worse. The boy could see that this was so. But no matter how little they had now, his uncle said, their reward in the end was the Lord Jesus Himself, the bread of life!

The boy would have a hideous vision of himself sitting forever with his great-uncle on a green bank, full and sick, staring at a broken fish and a multiplied loaf.

His uncle had been in the asylum four years because it had taken him four years to understand that the way for him to get out was to stop prophesying on the ward. It had taken him four years to discover what the boy felt he himself would have discovered in no time at all. But at least in the asylum the old man had learned caution and when he got out, he put everything he had learned to the service of his cause. He proceeded about the Lord's business like an experienced crook. He had given the sister up but he intended to help her boy. He planned to kidnap the child and keep him long enough to baptize him and instruct him in the facts of his Redemption and he mapped out his plan to the last detail and carried it out exactly.

Tarwater liked this part best because in spite of himself he had to admire his uncle's craft. The old man had persuaded Buford Munson to send his daughter in to get a job cooking for the sister and with the girl once in the house, he had been able to find out what he needed to know. He learned that there were two children now instead of one and that his sister sat in her nightgown all day drinking whiskey out of a medicine bottle. While Luella Munson washed and cooked and took care of the children, his sister lay on the bed sipping from the bottle and reading books that she had to buy fresh every night from the drugstore. But the principle reason the kidnapping had been so easy was because his great-uncle had had the full cooperation of the schoolteacher himself, a thin boy with a boney pale face and a pair of gold-rimmed spectacles that were always falling down his nose.

The two of them, the old man said, had liked each other from the first. The day he had gone to do the kidnapping, the husband was away on business and the sister, shut up in her room with the bottle, didn't even know the time of day. All the old man had done was to walk in and tell Luella Munson that his nephew was going off to spend a few days with him in the country and then he had gone out to the back yard and spoken to the schoolteacher who had been digging holes and lining them with broken glass.

He and the schoolteacher had taken the train as far as the junction and had walked the rest of the way to Powderhead. The old man had explained to him that he was not taking him on this trip for pleasure but because the Lord had sent him to do it, to

see that he was born again and instructed in his Redemption. All these facts were new to the schoolteacher, for his parents had never taught him anything, old Tarwater said, except not to wet the bed.

In four days the old man taught him what was
necessary to know and baptized him. He made him
understand that his true father was the Lord and not
the simpleton in town and that he would have to
lead a secret life in Jesus until the day came when
he would be able to bring the rest of his family
around to repentance. He had made him understand
that on the last day it would be his destiny to rise in
glory in the Lord Jesus. Since this was the first time
anybody had bothered to tell these facts to the
schoolteacher, he could not hear too much of them,
and as he had never seen woods before or been in
a boat or caught a fish or walked on roads that were
not paved, they did all those things too and, his uncle
said, he even allowed him to plow. His sallow face
had become bright in four days. At this point Tarwater would begin to weary of the story.

The schoolteacher had spent four days in the clearing because his mother had not missed him for three
days and when Luella Munson had mentioned where
he had gone, she had to wait another day before his
father came home and she could send him after the
child. She would not come herself, the old man said,
for fear the wrath of God would strike her at Powderhead and she would not be able to get back to the
city again. She had wired the schoolteacher's father

and when the simpleton arrived at the clearing, the schoolteacher was in despair at having to leave. The light had left his eyes. He had gone but the old man insisted that he had been able to tell by the look on his face that he would never be the same boy again.

"If he didn't say he didn't want to go, you can't be sure he didn't," Tarwater would say contentiously.

"Then why did he try to come back?" the old man asked. "Answer me that. Why one week later did he run away and try to find his way back and got his picture in the paper when the state patrol found him in the woods? I ask you why. Tell me that if you know so much."

"Because here was less bad than there," Tarwater said. "Less bad don't mean good, it only means better-than."

"He tried to come back," his uncle said slowly, emphasizing each word, "to hear more about God his Father, more about Jesus Christ Who had died to redeem him and more of the Truth I could tell him."

"Well go on," Tarwater would say irritably, "get on with the rest of it." The story always had to be taken to completion. It was like a road that the boy had travelled on so often that half the time he didn't look where they were going, and when at certain points he would become aware where they were, he would be surprised to see that the old man had not got farther on with it. Sometimes his uncle would lag at one point as if he didn't want to face what was coming and then when he finally came to it, he would try to get past it in a rush. At such points, Tarwater plagued him for details. "Tell about when he came when he was fourteen years old and had already decided none of it was true and he give you all that sass."

"Bah," the old man would say. "He was living in confusion. I don't say it was his fault then. They told him I was a crazy man. But I'll tell you one thing: he never believed them neither. They kept him from believing me but I kept him from believing them and he never took on none of their ways though he took on worse ones. And when he got shut of the three of them in that crash, nobody was gladder than he was. Then he turned his mind to raising you. Said he was going to give you every advantage, every advantage." The old man snorted. "You have me to thank for saving you from those advantages."

The boy looked off into the distance as though he were staring blankly at his invisible advantages.

"When he got shut of the three of them in that crash, this was the first place he came. On the very day they were killed he came out here to tell me. Straight out here. Yes sir," the old man said with the greatest satisfaction, "straight out here. He hadn't seen me in years but this is where he came. I was the one he came to. I was the one he wanted to see. Me. I had never left his mind. I had taken my seat in it."

"You skipped all that part about how he came when he was fourteen and give you all that sass," Tarwater said.

"It was sass he had got from them," the old man

said. "Just parrot-mouthing all they had ever said about how I was a crazy man. The truth was even if they told him not to believe what I had taught him, he couldn't forget it. He never could forget that there was a chance that that simpleton was not his only father. I planted the seed in him and it was there for good. Whether anybody liked it or not."

"It fell amongst cockles," Tarwater said. "Say the sass."

"It fell in deep," the old man said, "or else after that crash he wouldn't have come out here hunting me."

"He only wanted to see if you were still crazy," the boy offered.

"The day may come," his great-uncle said slowly, "when a pit opens up inside you and you know some things you never known before," and he would give him such a prescient piercing look that the child would turn his face away, scowling fiercely.

His great-uncle had gone to live with the schoolteacher and as soon as he had got there, he had baptized Tarwater, practically under the schoolteacher's nose and the schoolteacher had made a blasphemous joke of it. But the old man could never tell this straight through. He always had to back up and tell why he had gone to live with the schoolteacher in the first place. He had gone for three reasons. One, he said, because he knew the schoolteacher wanted him. He was the only person in the schoolteacher's life who had ever taken two steps out of his way in his behalf.

And two, because his nephew was the proper person to bury him and he wanted to have it understood with him how he wanted it done. And three, because the old man meant to see that Tarwater was baptized.

"I know all that," the boy would say, "get on with the rest of it."

"After the three of them perished and the house was his, he cleared it out," old Tarwater said. "He moved every stick of furniture out of it except a table and a chair or two and a bed or two and the crib he bought for you. Taken down all the pictures and all the curtains and taken up all the rugs. Even burned up all his mother's and sister's and the simpleton's clothes, didn't want a thing of theirs around. It wasn't anything left but books and papers that he had collected. Papers everywhere," the old man said. "Every room looked like the inside of a bird's nest. I came a few days after the crash and when he saw me standing there, he was glad to see me. His eyes lit up. He was glad to see me. 'Ha,' he said, 'my house is swept and garnished and here are the seven other devils, all rolled into one!'" The old man slapped his knee with pleasure.

"It don't sound to me like . . ."

"No, he didn't say so," he uncle said, "but I ain't an idiot."

"If he didn't say so you can't be sure."

"I'm as sure," his uncle said, "as I am that this here," and he held up his hand, every short thick finger stretched rigid in front of Tarwater's face, "is my hand and not yours." There was something final in this that always made the boy's impudence subside.

"Well get on with it," he would say. "If you don't make haste, you'll never get to where he blasphemed at."

"He was glad to see me," his uncle said. "He opened the door with all that house full of paper-trash behind him and there I stood and he was glad to see me. It was all underneath his face."

"What did he say?" Tarwater asked.

"He looked at my satchel," the old man said, "and he said, 'Uncle, you can't live with me. I know exactly what you want but I'm going to raise this child my way.'"

These words of the schoolteacher's had always caused a quick charge of excitement to race through Tarwater, an almost sensuous satisfaction. "It might have sounded to you like he was glad to see you," he said. "It don't sound that way to me."

"He wasn't but twenty-four years old," the old man said. "His expression hadn't even set on his face yet. I could still see the seven-year-old boy that had gone off with me, except that now he had a pair of black-rimmed glasses and a nose big enough to hold them up. The size of his eyes had shrunk because his face had grown but it was the same face all right. You could see behind it to what he really wanted to say. When he came out here later to get you back after I had stolen you, it was already set. It was as set then as the outside of a penitentiary but not now when I'm telling you about. Then it wasn't set and I could see he wanted me. Else why had he come out to Powderhead to tell me they were all dead? I ask you that? He could have let me alone."

The boy couldn't answer.

"Anyway," the old man said, "what all he gone on and done proved he wanted me right then because he took me in. He looked at my satchel and I said, 'I'm on your charity,' and he said, 'I'm sorry, Uncle. You can't live with me and ruin another child's life. This one is going to be brought up to live in the real world. He's going to be brought up to expect exactly what he can do for himself. He's going to be his own saviour. He's going to be free!' " The old man turned his head to the side and spit. "Free," he said. "He was full of such-like phrases. But then I said it. I said what changed his mind."

The boy sighed at this. The old man considered it his master stroke. He had said, "I never come to live with you. I come to die!"

"And you should have seen his face," he said. "He looked like he'd been pushed all of a sudden from behind. He hadn't cared if the other three were wiped out but when he thought of me going, it was like he was losing somebody for the first time. He stood there staring at me." And once, only once, the old man had leaned forward and said to Tarwater, in a voice that could no longer contain the pleasure of its secret, "He loved me like a daddy and he was ashamed of it!"

The boy's face had remained unmoved. "Yes," he said, "and you had told him a bare-face lie. You never had no intention of dying."

"I was sixty-nine years of age," his uncle said. "I could have died the next day as well as not. No man knows the hour of his death. I didn't have my life in front of me. It was not a lie, it was only a speculation. I told him, I said, 'I may live two months or two days.' And I had on my clothes that I bought to be buried in—all new."

"Ain't it that same suit you got on now?" the boy asked indignantly, pointing to the threadbare knee. "Ain't it that one you got on yourself right now?"

"I may live two months or two days, I said to him," his uncle said.

Or ten years or twenty, Tarwater thought.

"Oh it was a shock to him," the old man said.

It might have been a shock, the boy thought, but he wasn't all that sorry about it. The schoolteacher had merely said, "So I'm to put you away, Uncle? All right, I'll put you away. I'll do it with pleasure. I'll put you away for good and all," but the old man insisted that his words were one thing and his actions and the look on his face another.

His great-uncle had not been in the nephew's house ten minutes before he had baptized Tarwater. They had gone into the room where the crib was with Tarwater in it and as the old man looked at him for the first time—a wizened grey-faced scrawny sleeping baby—the voice of the Lord had come to him and said: HERE IS THE PROPHET TO TAKE YOUR PLACE. BAPTIZE HIM.

That? the old man had asked, that wizened grey-faced . . . and then as he wondered how he could baptize him with the nephew standing there, the Lord had sent the paper boy to knock on the door and the schoolteacher had gone to answer it.

When he came back in a few minutes, his uncle was holding Tarwater in one hand and with the other he was pouring water over his head out of the bottle that had been on the table by the crib. He had pulled off the nipple and stuck it in his pocket. He was just finishing the words of baptism as the schoolteacher came back in the door and he had had to laugh when he looked up and saw his nephew's face. It looked hacked, the old man said. Not even angry at first, just hacked.

Old Tarwater had said, "He's been born again and there ain't a thing you can do about it," and then he had seen the rage rise in the nephew's face and had seen him try to conceal it.

"Time has passed you by, Uncle," the nephew said. "That can't even irritate me. That only makes me laugh," and he laughed, a short forced bark, but the old man said his face was mottled. "Just as well you did it now," he said. "If you had got me when I was seven days instead of seven years, you might not have ruined my life."

"If it's ruined," the old man said, "it wasn't me that ruined it."

"Oh yes it was," the nephew said, advancing across the room, his face very red. "You're too blind to see what you did to me. A child can't defend himself. Children are cursed with believing. You pushed me out of the real world and I stayed out of it until I didn't know which was which. You infected me with your idiot hopes, your foolish violence. I'm not always myself, I'm not al . . ." but he stopped. He wouldn't admit what the old man knew. "There's nothing wrong with me," he said. "I've straightened the tangle you made. Straightened it by pure will power. I've made myself straight."

"You see," the old man said, "he admitted himself the seed was still in him."

Old Tarwater had laid the baby back in the crib but the nephew took him out again, a peculiar smile, the old man said, stiffening on his face. "If one baptism is good, two will be better," he said and he had turned Tarwater over and poured what was left in the bottle over his bottom and said the words of baptism again. Old Tarwater had stood there, aghast at this blasphemy. "Now Jesus has a claim on both ends," the nephew said.

The old man had roared, "Blasphemy never changed a plan of the Lord's!"

"And the Lord hasn't changed any of mine either," said the nephew coolly and put the baby back.

"And what did I do?" Tarwater asked.

"You didn't do nothing," the old man said as if what he did or didn't do was of no consequence whatsoever.

"It was me that was the prophet," the boy said sullenly.

"You didn't even know what was going on," his uncle said.

"Oh yes I did," the child said. "I was laying there thinking."

His uncle would ignore this and go on. He had thought for a while that by living with the schoolteacher, he might convince him again of all that he had convinced him of when he had kidnapped him as a child and he had had hope of it up until the time when the schoolteacher showed him the study he had written of him for the magazine. Then the old man had realized at last that there was no hope of his doing anything for the schoolteacher. He had failed the schoolteacher's mother and he had failed the schoolteacher, and now there was nothing to do but try to save Tarwater from being brought up by a fool. In this he had not failed.

The boy felt that the schoolteacher could have made more of an effort to get him back. He had come out and got shot in the leg and the ear but if he had used his head, he might have avoided that and got him back at the same time. "Why didn't he bring the law out here and get me back?" he had asked.

"You want to know why?" his uncle said. "Well I'll tell you why. I'll tell you exactly why. It was because he found you a heap of trouble. He wanted it all in his head. You can't change a child's pants in your head."

The boy would think: but if the schoolteacher hadn't written that piece on him, we might all three be living in town right now.

When the old man had read the piece in the schoolteacher magazine, he had at first not recognized who it was the schoolteacher was writing about, who the type was that was almost extinct. He had sat down to read the piece, full of pride that his nephew had succeeded in having a composition printed in a magazine. He had handed it carelessly to his uncle and said he might want to glance over it and the old man had sat down at once at the kitchen table and commenced to read it. He recalled that the schoolteacher had kept passing by the kitchen door to witness how he was taking the piece.

About the middle of it, old Tarwater had begun to think that he was reading about someone he had once known or at least someone he had dreamed about, for the figure was strangely familiar. "This fixation of being called by the Lord had its origin in insecurity. He needed the assurance of a call and so he called himself," he read. The schoolteacher kept passing by the door, passing and repassing, and finally he came in and sat down quietly on the other side of the small white metal table. When the old man looked up, the schoolteacher smiled. It was a very slight smile, the slightest that would do for any occasion. The old man knew from the smile who it was he had been reading about.

For the length of a minute, he could not move. He felt he was tied hand and foot inside the schoolteacher's head, a space as bare and neat as the cell in the asylum, and was shrinking, drying up to fit it. His eyeballs swerved from side to side as if he were pinned in a strait jacket again. Jonah, Ezekiel, Daniel, he was at that moment all of them—the swallowed, the lowered, the enclosed.

The nephew, his smile still fixed, reached across the table and put his hand on the old man's wrist in a gesture of pity. "You've got to be born again, Uncle," he said, "by your own efforts, back to the real world where there's no saviour but yourself."

The old man's tongue lay in his mouth like a stone but his heart began to swell. His prophet's blood surged in him, surged to floodtide for a miraculous release, though his face remained shocked, expressionless. The nephew patted his huge clenched fist and got up and left the kitchen, bearing away his smile of triumph.

The next morning when he went to the crib to give the baby his bottle, he found nothing in it but the blue magazine with the old man's message scrawled on the back of it: THE PROPHET I RAISE UP OUT OF THIS BOY WILL BURN YOUR EYES CLEAN.

"It was me could act," the old man said, "not him. He could never take action. He could only get everything inside his head and grind it to nothing. But I

acted. And because I acted, you sit here in freedom,
you sit here a rich man, knowing the Truth, in the
freedom of the Lord Jesus Christ."

The boy would move his thin shoulder blades irritably as if he were shifting the burden of Truth like
a cross on his back. "He came out here and got shot
to get me back," he said obstinately.

"If he had really wanted you back, he could have
got you," the old man said. "He could have had the
law out here after me or got me put back in the
asylum. There was plenty he could have done, but
what happened to him was that welfare-woman. She
persuaded him to have one of his own and let you
go, and he was easy persuaded. And that one," the
old man would say, beginning to brood on the schoolteacher's child again, "that one—the Lord gave him
one he couldn't corrupt." And then he would grip
the boy's shoulder and put a fierce pressure on it.
"And if I don't get him baptized, it'll be for you to
do," he said. "I enjoin you to do it, boy."

Nothing irritated the boy so much as this. "I take
my orders from the Lord," he would say in an ugly
voice, trying to pry the fingers out of his shoulder.
"Not from you."

"The Lord will give them to you," the old man said,
gripping his shoulder tighter.

"He had to change that one's pants and he done
it," Tarwater muttered.

"He had the welfare-woman to do it for him," his
uncle said. "She had to be good for something, but

you can bet she ain't still around there. Bernice Bishop!" he said as if he found this the most idiotic name in the language. "Bernice Bishop!"

The boy had sense enough to know that he had been betrayed by the schoolteacher and he did not mean to go to his house until daylight, when he could see behind and before him. "I ain't going there until daylight," he said suddenly to Meeks. "You needn't to stop there because I ain't getting out there."

Meeks leaned casually against the door of the car, driving with half his attention and giving the other half to Tarwater. "Son," he said, "I'm not going to be a preacher to you. I'm not going to tell you not to lie. I ain't going to tell you nothing impossible. All I'm going to tell you is this: don't lie when you don't have to. Else when you do have to, nobody'll believe you. You don't have to lie to me. I know exactly what you done." A shaft of light plunged through the car window and he looked to the side and saw the white face beside him, staring up with soot-colored eyes.

"How do you know?" the boy asked.

Meeks smiled with pleasure. "Because I done the same thing myself once," he said.

Tarwater caught hold of the sleeve of the salesman's coat and gave it a quick pull. "On the Day of Judgment," he said, "me and you will rise and say we done it!"

Meeks looked at him again with one eyebrow

cocked at the same angle he wore his hat. "Will we?"
he asked. Then he said, "What line you gonna get
into, boy?"

"What line?"

"What you going to do? What kind of *work?*"

"I know everything but the machines," Tarwater
said, sitting back again. "My great-uncle learnt me
everything but first I have to find out how much of
it is true." They were entering the dilapidated out-
skirts of the city where wooden buildings leaned together and an occasional dim light lit up a faded sign
advertising some remedy or other.

"What line was your great-uncle in?" Meeks asked.

"He was a prophet," the boy said.

"Is that right?" Meeks asked and his shoulders
jumped several times as if they were going to leap
over his head. "Who'd he prophesy to?"

"To me," Tarwater said. "Nobody else would listen
to him and there wasn't anybody else for me to listen
to. He grabbed me away from this other uncle, my
only blood connection now, so as to save me from
running to doom."

"You were a captive audience," Meeks said. "And
now you're coming to town to run to doom with the
rest of us, huh?"

The boy didn't answer at once. Then he said in a
guarded tone, "I ain't said what I'm going to do."

"You ain't sure about what all this great-uncle of
yours told you, are you?" Meeks asked. "You figure
he might have got aholt to some misinformation."

Tarwater looked away, out the window, at the brittle forms of the houses. He was holding both arms close to his sides as if he were cold. "I'll find out," he said.

"Well how now?" Meeks asked.

The dark city was unfolding on either side of them and they were approaching a low circle of light in the distance. "I mean to wait and see what happens," he said after a moment.

"And suppose nothing don't happen?" Meeks asked.

The circle of light became huge and they swung into the center of it and stopped. It was a gaping concrete mouth with two red gas pumps set in front of it and a small glass office toward the back. "I say suppose nothing don't happen?" Meeks repeated.

The boy looked at him darkly, remembering the silence after his great uncle's death.

"Well?" Meeks said.

"Then I'll make it happen," he said. "I can act."

"Attaboy," Meeks said. He opened the car door and put his leg out while he continued to observe his rider. Then he said, "Wait a minute. I got to call my girl."

A man was asleep in a chair tilted against the outside wall of the glass office and Meeks went inside without waking him up. For a minute Tarwater only craned his neck out the window. Then he got out and went to the office door to watch Meeks use the machine. It sat, small and black, in the center of a cluttered desk which Meeks sat down on as if it had been his own. The room was lined with automobile tires and had a concrete and rubber smell. Meeks took the machine in two parts and held one part to his head while he circled with his finger on the other part. Then he sat waiting, swinging his foot, while the horn buzzed in his ear. After a minute an acid smile began to eat at the corners of his mouth and he said, drawing in his breath, "Heythere, Sugar, hyer you?" and Tarwater, from where he stood in the door, heard an actual woman's voice, like one coming from beyond the grave, say, "Why Sugar, is that reely you?" and Meeks said it was him in the same old flesh and made an appointment with her in ten minutes.

Tarwater stood awestruck in the doorway. Meeks put the telephone together and then he said in a sly voice, "Now why don't you call your uncle?" and watched the boy's face change, the eyes swerve suspiciously to the side and the flesh drop around the boney mouth.

"I'll speak with him soon enough," he muttered, but he kept looking at the black coiled machine, fascinated. "How do you use it?" he asked.

"You dial it like I did. Call your uncle," Meeks urged.

"No, that woman is waiting on you," Tarwater said.

"Let 'er wait," Meeks said. "That's what she knows how to do best."

The boy approached it, taking out the card he had written the number on. He put his finger on the dial and began gingerly to turn it.

"Great God," Meeks said and took the receiver off the hook and put it in his hand and thrust his hand to his ear. He dialed the number for him and then pushed him down in the office chair to wait but Tarwater stood up again, slightly crouched, holding the buzzing horn to his head, while his heart began to kick viciously at his chest wall.

"It don't speak," he murmured.

"Give him time," Meeks said, "maybe he don't like to get up in the middle of the night."

The buzzing continued for a minute and then stopped abruptly. Tarwater stood speechless, holding the earpiece tight against his head, his face rigid as if he were afraid that the Lord might be about to speak to him over the machine. All at once he heard what sounded like heavy breathing in his ear.

"Ask for your party," Meeks prompted. "How do you expect to get your party if you don't ask for him?"

The boy remained exactly as he was, saying nothing.

"I told you to ask for your party," Meeks said irritably. "Ain't you got good sense?"

"I want to speak with my uncle," Tarwater whispered.

There was a silence over the telephone but it was not a silence that seemed to be empty. It was the kind where the breath is drawn in and held. Suddenly the boy realized that it was the schoolteacher's child on the other side of the machine. The white-haired, blunted face rose before him. He said in a furious shaking voice, "I want to speak with my uncle. Not you!"

The heavy breathing began again as if in answer. It was a kind of bubbling noise, the kind of noise someone would make who was struggling to breathe in water. In a second it faded away. The horn of the machine dropped out of Tarwater's hand. He stood there blankly as if he had received a revelation he could not yet decipher. He seemed to have been stunned by some deep internal blow that had not yet made its way to the surface of his mind.

Meeks picked up the earpiece and listened but there was no sound. He put it back on the hook and said, "Come on. I ain't got this kind of time." He gave the stupefied boy a shove and they left, driving off into the city again. Meeks told him to learn to work every machine he saw. The greatest invention of man, he said, was the wheel and he asked Tarwater if he had ever thought how things were before it was a wheel, but the boy didn't answer him. He didn't even appear to be listening. He sat slightly forward and from time to time his lips moved as if he were speaking silently with himself.

"Well, it was terrible," Meeks said sourly. He knew the boy didn't have any uncle at any such respectable address and to prove it, he turned down the street the uncle was supposed to live on and drove slowly past the small shapes of squat houses until he found the number, visible in phosphorescent letters on a small stick set on the edge of the grass plot. He stopped the car and said, "Okay, kiddo, that's it."

"That's what?" Tarwater mumbled.

"That's your uncle's house," Meeks said.

The boy grabbed the edge of the window with both hands and stared out at what appeared to be only a black shape crouched in a greater darkness a little distance away. "I told you I wasn't going there until daylight," he said angrily, "go on."

"You're going there right now," Meeks said. "Because I ain't getting stuck with you. You can't go with me where I'm going."

"I ain't getting out here," the boy said.

Meeks reached across him and opened the car door. "So long, son," he said, "if you get real hungry by next week, you can contack me from that card and we might make a deal."

The boy gave him one white-faced outraged look and flung himself from the car. He moved up the short concrete walk to the doorstep and sat down abruptly, absorbed into the darkness. Meeks pulled the car door shut. His face hung for a moment watching the barely visible outline of the boy's shape on the step. Then he drew back and drove on. He won't come to no good end, he said to himself.

III

TARWATER sat in the corner of the doorstep, scowling in the dark as the car disappeared down the block. He did not look up at the sky but he was unpleasantly aware of the stars. They seemed to be holes in his skull through which some distant unmoving light was watching him. It was as if he were alone in the presence of an immense silent eye. He had an intense desire to make himself known to the schoolteacher at once, to tell him what he had done and why and to be congratulated by him. At the same time, his deep suspicion of the man continued to work in him. He tried to bring the schoolteacher's face again to mind, but all he could manage was the face of the seven-year-old boy the old man had kidnapped. He stared at it boldly, hardening himself for the encounter.

Then he rose and faced the heavy brass knocker on the door. He touched it and jerked his hand away, burnt by a metallic coldness. He looked quickly over his shoulder. The houses across the street formed a dark jagged wall. The quiet seemed palpable, waiting. It seemed almost to be waiting patiently, biding its time until it should reveal itself and demand to be named. He turned back to the cold knocker and grabbed it and shattered the silence as if it were a personal enemy. The noise filled his head. He was aware of nothing but the racket he was making.

He beat louder and louder, bamming at the same time with his free fist until he felt he was shaking the house. The empty street echoed with his blows. He stopped once to get his breath and then began again, kicking the door frenziedly with the blunt toe of his heavy work shoe. Nothing happened. Finally he stopped and the implacable silence descended around him, immune to his fury. A mysterious dread filled him. His whole body felt hollow as if he had been lifted like Habakkuk by the hair of his head, borne swiftly through the night and set down in the place of his mission. He had a sudden foreboding that he was about to step into a trap laid for him by the old man. He half-turned to run.

At once the glass panels on either side of the door filled with light. There was a click and the knob turned. Tarwater jerked his hands up automatically as if he were pointing an invisible gun and his uncle, who had opened the door, jumped back at the sight of him.

The image of the seven-year-old boy disappeared forever from Tarwater's mind. His uncle's face was so familiar to him that he might have seen it every day of his life. He steadied himself and shouted, "My great-uncle is dead and burnt, just like you would have burnt him yourself!"

The schoolteacher remained absolutely still as if he thought that by looking long enough his hallucination would disappear. He had been roused by the vibration in the house and had run, half-asleep, to the door. His face was like the face of a sleep-walker who wakes and sees some horror of his dreams take shape before him. After a moment he muttered, "Wait here, deaf," and turned and went quickly out of the hall. He was barefooted and in his pajamas. He came back almost at once, plugging something into his ear. He had thrust on the black-rimmed glasses and he was sticking a metal box into the waist-band of his pajamas. This was joined by a cord to the plug in his ear. For an instant the boy had the thought that his head ran by electricity. He caught Tarwater by the arm and pulled him into the hall under a lantern-shaped light that hung from the ceiling. The boy found himself scrutinized by two small drill-like eyes set in the depths of twin glass caverns. He drew away. Already he felt his privacy imperilled.

"My great-uncle is dead and burnt," he said again. "I was the only one there to do it and I done it. I done your work for you," and as he said the last, a perceptible trace of scorn crossed his face.

"Dead?" the schoolteacher said. "My uncle? The old man's dead?" he asked in a blank unbelieving tone. He caught Tarwater abruptly by the arms and stared into his face. In the depths of his eyes, the boy, shocked, saw an instant's stricken look, plain and awful. It vanished at once. The straight line of the schoolteacher's mouth began turning into a smile. "And how did he go—with his fist in the air?" he asked. "Did the Lord arrive for him in a chariot of fire?"

"He didn't have no warning," Tarwater said, suddenly breathless. "He was eating his breakfast and I never moved him from the table. I set him on fire where he was and the house with him."

The schoolteacher said nothing but the boy read in his look a doubt that this had happened, a suspicion that he dealt with an interesting liar.

"You can go there and see for yourself," Tarwater said. "He was too big to bury. I done it the quickest way."

His uncle's eyes had the look now of being trained on a fascinating problem. "How did you get here? How did you know this was where you belonged?" he asked.

The boy had expended all his energy announcing himself. He was suddenly blank and stunned and he remained stupidly silent. He had never been this tired before. He felt he was about to fall.

The schoolteacher waited, searching his face impatiently. Then his expression changed again. He tightened his grip on Tarwater's arm and his eyes turned, glowering, toward the front door, which was still open. "Is he out there?" he asked in a low enraged voice. "Is this one of his tricks? Is he out there waiting to sneak in a window and baptize Bishop while you're here baiting me? Is that his senile game this time?"

The boy blanched. In his mind's eye he saw the old man, a dark shape standing behind the corner of the house, restraining his wheezing breath while he waited impatiently for him to baptize the dim-witted child. He stared shocked at the schoolteacher's face. There was a wedge-shaped gash in his new uncle's ear. The sight of it brought old Tarwater so close that the boy thought he could hear him laugh. With a terrible clarity he saw that the schoolteacher was no more than a decoy the old man had set up to lure him to the city to do his unfinished business.

His eyes began to burn in his fierce fragile face. A new energy seized him. "He's dead," he said. "You can't be any deader than he is. He's reduced to ashes. He don't even have a cross set up over him. If it's anything left of him, the buzzards wouldn't have it and the bones the dogs'll carry off. That's how dead he is."

The schoolteacher winced, but almost at once he was smiling again. He held Tarwater's arms tightly and peered into his face as if he were beginning to see a solution, one that intrigued him with its symmetry and rightness. "It's a perfect irony," he murmured, "a perfect irony that you should have taken care of the matter in that way. He got what he deserved."

The boy's pride swelled. "I done the needful," he said.

"Everything he touched he warped," the schoolteacher said. "He lived a long and useless life and he did you a great injustice. It's a blessing he's dead at last. You could have had everything and you've had nothing. All that can be changed now. Now you belong to someone who can help you and understand you." His eyes were alight with pleasure. "It's not too late for me to make a man of you!"

The boy's face darkened. His expression hardened until it was a fortress wall to keep his thoughts from being exposed; but the schoolteacher did not notice any change. He gazed through the actual insignificant boy before him to an image of him that he held fully developed in his mind.

"You and I will make up for lost time," he said. "We'll get you started now in the right direction."

Tarwater was not looking at him. His neck had suddenly snapped forward and he was staring straight ahead over the schoolteacher's shoulder. He heard a faint familiar sound of heavy breathing. It was closer to him than the beating of his own heart. His eyes widened and an inner door in them opened in preparation for some inevitable vision.

The small white-haired boy shambled into the back of the hall and stood peering forward at the stranger. He had on the bottoms to a pair of blue pajamas drawn up as high as they would go, the string tied over his chest and then again, harness-like, around his neck to keep them on. His eyes were slightly sunken beneath his forehead and his cheekbones were lower than they should have been. He stood there, dim and ancient, like a child who had been a child for centuries.

Tarwater clenched his fists. He stood like one condemned, waiting at the spot of execution. Then the revelation came, silent, implacable, direct as a bullet. He did not look into the eyes of any fiery beast or see a burning bush. He only knew, with a certainty sunk in despair, that he was expected to baptize the child he saw and begin the life his great-uncle had prepared him for. He knew that he was called to be a prophet and that the ways of his prophecy would not be remarkable. His black pupils, glassy and still, reflected depth on depth his own stricken image of himself, trudging into the distance in the bleeding stinking mad shadow of Jesus, until at last he received his reward, a broken fish, a multiplied loaf. The Lord out of dust had created him, had made him blood and nerve and mind, had made him to bleed and weep and think, and set him in a world of loss and fire all to baptize one idiot child that He need not have created in the first place and to cry out a gospel just as foolish. He tried to shout, "NO!" but it was like trying to shout in his sleep. The sound was saturated in silence, lost.

His uncle put a hand on his shoulder and shook him slightly to penetrate his inattention. "Listen boy," he said, "getting out from under the old man is just like coming out of the darkness into the light. You're going to have a chance now for the first time in your life. A chance to develop into a useful man, a chance to use your talents, to do what you want to do and not what he wanted—whatever idiocy it was."

The boy's eyes were focussed beyond him, the pupils dilated. The schoolteacher turned his head to see what it was that was keeping him from being responsive. His own face tightened. The little boy was creeping forward, grinning.

"That's only Bishop," he said. "He's not all right. Don't mind him. All he can do is stare at you and he's very friendly. He stares at everything that way." His hand tightened on the boy's shoulder and his mouth stretched painfully. "All the things that I would do for him—if it were any use—I'll do for you," he said. "Now do you see why I'm so glad to have you here?"

The boy heard nothing he said. The muscles in his neck stood out like cables. The dim-witted child was not five feet from him and was coming every instant closer with his lop-sided smile. Suddenly he knew that the child *recognized* him, that the old man himself had primed him from on high that here was the forced servant of God come to see that he was born again. The little boy was sticking out his hand to touch him.

"Git!" Tarwater screamed. His arm shot out like a whip and knocked the hand away. The child let out a bellow startlingly loud. He clambered up his father's leg, pulling himself up by the schoolteacher's pajama coat until he was almost on his shoulder.

"All right, all right," the schoolteacher said, "there, there, shut up, it's all right, he didn't mean to hit you," and he righted the child on his back and tried to slide him off but the little boy hung on, thrusting his head against his father's neck and never taking his eyes off Tarwater.

The boy had a vision of the schoolteacher and his child as inseparably joined. The schoolteacher's face was red and pained. The child might have been a deformed part of himself that had been accidentally revealed.

"You'll get used to him," he said.

"No!" the boy shouted.

It was like a shout that had been waiting, straining to burst out. "I won't get used to him! I won't have anything to do with him!" He clenched his fist and lifted it. "I won't have anything to do with him!" he shouted and the words were clear and positive and defiant like a challenge hurled in the face of his silent adversary.

TWO

IV

AFTER four days of Tarwater, the schoolteacher's enthusiasm had passed. He would admit no more than that. It had passed the first day and had been succeeded by determination, and while he knew that determination was a less powerful tool, he thought that in this case, it was the one best fitted for the job. It had taken him barely half a day to find out that the old man had made a wreck of the boy and that what was called for was a monumental job of reconstruction. The first day enthusiasm had given him energy but ever since, determination had exhausted him.

Although it was only eight o'clock in the evening,

he had put Bishop to bed and had told the boy that he could go to his room and read. He had bought him books, among other things still ignored. Tarwater had gone to his room and had closed the door, not saying whether he intended to read or not, and Rayber was in bed for the night, lying too exhausted to sleep, watching the late evening light fade through the hedge that grew in front of his window. He had left his hearing aid on so that if the boy tried to escape, he would hear and could go after him. For the last two days he had looked poised to leave, and not simply to leave but to be gone, silently and in the night when he would not be followed. This was the fourth night and the schoolteacher lay thinking, with a wry expression on his face, how it differed from the first.

The first night he had sat until daylight by the side of the bed where, still dressed, the boy had fallen. He had sat there, his eyes shining, like a man who sits before a treasure he is not yet convinced is real. His eyes had moved over and over the sprawled thin figure which had appeared lost in an exhaustion so profound that it seemed doubtful it would ever move again. As he followed the outline of the face, he had realized with an intense stab of joy that his nephew looked enough like him to be his son. The heavy work shoes, the worn overalls, the atrocious stained hat filled him with pain and pity. He thought of his poor sister. The only real pleasure she had had in her life was the time she had had the lover who had given her this child, the hollow-cheeked boy who had come from the country to study divinity but whose mind Rayber (a graduate student at the time) had seen at once was too good for that. He had befriended him, had helped him to discover himself and then to discover her. He had engineered their meeting purposely and then had observed to his delight how it prospered and how the relationship developed them both. If there had been no accident, he felt sure the boy would have become completely stable. As it was, after the calamity he had killed himself, a prey to morbid guilt. He had come to Rayber's apartment and had stood confronting him with the gun. He saw again the long brittle face as raw red as if a blast of fire had singed the skin off it and the eyes that had seemed burnt too. He had not felt they were entirely human eyes. They were the eyes of repentence and lacked all dignity. The boy had looked at him for what seemed an age but was perhaps only a second, then he had turned without a word and left and killed himself as soon as he reached his own room.

When Rayber had first opened the door in the middle of the night and had seen Tarwater's face—white, drawn by some unfathomable hunger and pride—he had remained for an instant frozen before what might have been a mirror thrust toward him in a nightmare. The face before him was his own, but the eyes were not his own. They were the student's eyes, singed with guilt. He had left the door hurriedly to get his glasses and his hearing aid.

As he sat that first night by the bed, he had recognized something rigid and recalcitrant about the boy even in repose. He lay with his teeth bared and the hat clenched in his fist like a weapon. Rayber's conscience smote him that all these years he had left him to his fate, that he had not gone back and saved him. His throat had tightened, his eyes had begun to ache. He had vowed to make it up to him now, to lavish on him everything he would have lavished on his own child if he had had one who would have known the difference.

The next morning while Tarwater was still asleep, he had rushed out and bought him a decent suit, a plaid shirt, socks, and a red leather cap. He wanted him to have new clothes to wake up to, new clothes to indicate a new life.

After four days they were still untouched in the box on a chair in the room. The boy had looked at them as if the suggestion he put them on were equal to asking that he appear naked.

It was apparent from everything he did and said exactly who had brought him up. At every turn an almost uncontrollable fury would rise in Rayber at the brand of independence the old man had wrought —not a constructive independence but one that was irrational, backwoods, and ignorant. After Rayber had rushed back with the clothes, he had gone to the bed and put his hand on the still sleeping boy's forehead and decided that he had a fever and should not get up. He had prepared a breakfast on a tray and brought it to the room. When he appeared in the door with it, Bishop at his side, Tarwater was sitting up in the bed, in the act of shaking out his hat and putting it on. Rayber had said, "Don't you want to hang up your hat and stay a while?" and had given him such a smile of welcome and good will as he thought had possibly never been turned on him before.

The boy, with no look of appreciation or even interest, had pulled the hat down farther on his head. His gaze had turned with a peculiar glare of recognition to Bishop. The child had on a black cowboy hat and he was gaping over the top of a trashbasket that he clasped to his stomach. He kept a rock in it. Rayber remembered that Bishop had caused the boy some disturbance the night before and he pushed him back with his free hand so that he could not get in. Then stepping into the room, he closed the door and locked it. Tarwater looked at the closed door darkly as if he continued to see the child through it, still clasping his trashbasket.

Rayber set the tray down across his knees and stood back scrutinizing him. The boy seemed barely aware that he was in the room. "That's your breakfast," his uncle said as if he might not be able to identify it. It was a bowl of dry cereal and a glass of milk. "I thought you'd better stay in bed today," he said. "You don't look too chipper." He pulled up a straight chair and sat down. "Now we can have a real talk," he said, his smile spreading. "It's high time we got to know each other."

No expression of approval or pleasure lightened the boy's face. He glanced at the breakfast but did not pick up the spoon. He began to look around the room. The walls were an insistent pink, the color chosen by Rayber's wife. He used it now for a store room. There were trunks in the corners with crates piled on top of them. On the mantel, besides medicine bottles and dead electric lightbulbs and some old match boxes, was a picture of her. The boy's attention paused there and the corner of his mouth twitched slightly as if in some kind of comic recognition. "The welfare woman," he said.

His uncle reddened. The tone he detected under this was old Tarwater's exactly. Without warning, irritation mounted in him. The old man might suddenly have obtruded his presence between them. He felt the same familiar fantastic anger, out of all proportion to its cause, that his uncle had always been able to stir in him. With an effort, he forced it out of his way. "That's my wife," he said, "but she doesn't live with us anymore. This is her old room you're in."

The boy picked up the spoon. "My great-uncle said she wouldn't hang around long," he said and began to eat rapidly as if he had established enough independence by this remark to eat somebody else's food. It was apparent from his expression that he found the quality of it poor.

Rayber sat and watched him, saying to himself in an effort to calm his irritation: this child hasn't had a chance, remember he hasn't had a chance. "God only knows what the old fool has told you and taught you!" he said with a sudden explosive force. "God only knows!"

The boy stopped eating and looked at him sharply. Then after a second he said, "He ain't had no effect on me," and returned to his eating.

"He did you a terrible injustice," Rayber said, wishing to impress this on him as often as he could. "He kept you from having a normal life, from getting a decent education. He filled your head with God knows what rot!"

Tarwater continued to eat. Then with a stoney deliberateness, he looked up and his gaze fastened on the gash in his uncle's ear. Somewhere in the depths of his eyes a glint appeared. "Shot yer, didn't he?" he said.

Rayber took a package of cigarets from his shirt pocket and lit one, his motions inordinately slow from the effort he was making to calm himself. He blew the smoke straight into the boy's face. Then he tilted back in the chair and gave him a long hard look. The cigaret hanging from the corner of his mouth trembled. "Yes, he shot me," he said.

The glint in the boy's eyes followed the wires of the hearing aid down to the metal box stuck in his belt. "What you wired for?" he drawled. "Does your head light up?"

Rayber's jaw snapped and then relaxed. After a moment, after extending his arm stiffly and knocking the ash off his cigaret onto the floor, he replied that his head did not light up. "This is a hearing aid," he said patiently. "After the old man shot me I began to lose my hearing. I didn't have a gun when I went to get you back. If I'd stayed he would have killed me and I wouldn't have done you any good dead."

The boy continued to study the machine. His uncle's face might have been only an appendage to it. "You ain't done me no good alive neither," he remarked.

"Do you understand me?" Rayber persisted. "I didn't have a gun. He would have killed me. He was a mad man. The time when I can do you good is beginning now, and I want to help you. I want to make up for all those years."

For an instant the boy's eyes left the hearing aid and rested on his uncle's eyes. "Could have got you a gun and come back terreckly," he said.

Stricken by the distinct sound of betrayal in his voice, Rayber could not say a word. He looked at him helplessly. The boy returned to his eating.

Finally Rayber said, "Listen." He took hold of the fist with the spoon in it and held it. "I want you to understand. He was crazy and if he had killed me, you wouldn't have this place to come to now. I'm no fool. I don't believe in senseless sacrifice. A dead man is not going to do you any good, don't you know that? Now I can do something for you. Now I can make up for all the time we've lost. I can help correct what he's done to you, help you to correct it yourself." He kept hold of the fist all the while it was being drawn insistently back. "This is our problem together," he said, seeing himself so clearly in the face before him that he might have been beseeching his own image.

With a quick yank, Tarwater managed to free his hand. Then he gave the schoolteacher a long appraising look, tracing the line of his jaw, the two creases on either side of his mouth, the forehead extending into skull until it reached the pie-shaped hairline. He gazed briefly at the pained eyes behind his uncle's glasses, appearing to abandon a search for something that could not possibly be there. The glint in his eye fell on the metal box half-sticking out of Rayber's shirt. "Do you think in the box," he asked, "or do you think in your head?"

His uncle had wanted to tear the machine out of his ear and fling it against the wall. "It's because of you I can't hear!" he said, glaring at the impassive face. "It's because once I tried to help you!"

"You never helped me none."

"I can help you now," he said.

After a second he sank back in his chair. "Perhaps you're right," he said, letting his hands fall in a helpless gesture. "It·was my mistake. I should have gone back and killed him or let him kill me. Instead I let something in you be killed."

The boy put down his milk glass. "Nothing in me has been killed," he said in a positive voice, and then he added, "And you needn't to worry. I done your work for you. I tended to him. It was me put him away. I was drunk as a coot and I tended to him." He said it as if he were recalling the most vivid point in his history.

Rayber heard his own heart, magnified by the hearing aid, suddenly begin to pound like the works of a gigantic machine in his chest. The boy's delicate defiant face, his glowering eyes still shocked by some violent memory, brought back instantly to him the vision of himself when he was fourteen and had found his way to Powderhead to shout imprecations at the old man.

An insight came to him that he was not to question until the end. He understood that the boy was held in bondage by his great-uncle, that he suffered a terrible false guilt for burning and not burying him, and he saw that he was engaged in a desperate heroic struggle to free himself from the old man's ghostly grasp. He leaned forward and said in a voice so full of feeling that it was barely balanced, "Listen, listen Frankie," he said, "you're not alone any more. You have a friend. You have more than a friend now." He swallowed. "You have a father."

The boy turned very white. His eyes were blackened by the shadow of some unspeakable outrage. "I ain't ast for no father," he said and the sentence struck like a whip across his uncle's face. "I ain't ast for no father," he repeated. "I'm out of the womb of a whore. I was born in a wreck." He flung this forth as if he were declaring a royal birth. "And my name ain't Frankie. I go by Tarwater and . . ."

"Your mother was not a whore," the schoolteacher said angrily. "That's just some rot he's taught you. She was a good healthy American girl, just beginning to find herself when she was struck down. She was . . ."

"I ain't fixing to hang around here," the boy said, looking about him as if he might throw over the breakfast tray and jump out the window. "I only come to find out a few things and when I find them out, then I'm going."

"What did you come to find out?" the schoolteacher asked evenly. "I can help you. All I want to do is help you any way I can."

"I don't need noner yer help," the boy said, looking away.

His uncle felt something tightening around him like an invisible strait jacket. "How do you mean to find out if you don't have help?"

"I'll wait," he said, "and see what happens."

"And suppose," his uncle asked, "nothing happens?"

An odd smile, like some strange inverted sign of grief, came over the boy's face. "Then I'll make it happen," he said, "like I done before."

In four days nothing had happened and nothing had been made to happen. They had simply covered —the three of them—the entire city, walking and all night Rayber rewalked the same territory backwards in his sleep. It would not have been so tiring if he had not had Bishop. The child dragged backwards on his hand, always attracted by something

they had already passed. Every block or so he would
squat down to pick up a stick or a piece of trash and
have to be pulled up and along. Whereas Tarwater
was always slightly in advance of them, pushing forward on the scent of something. In four days they
had been to the art gallery and the movies, they had
toured department stores, ridden escalators, visited
the supermarkets, inspected the water works, the post
office, the railroad yards and the city hall. Rayber had
explained how the city was run and detailed the du-
ties of a good citizen. He had talked as much as he
had walked, and the boy for all the interest he showed
might have been the one who was deaf. Silent, he
viewed everything with the same noncommittal eye
as if he found nothing here worth holding his attention but must keep moving, must keep searching for
whatever it was that appeared just beyond his vision.

Once he had paused at a window where a small
red car turned slowly on a revolving platform. Seizing
on the display of interest, Rayber had said that perhaps when he was sixteen, he could have a car of his
own. It might have been the old man who had replied that he could walk on his two feet for nothing
without being beholden. Rayber had never, even
when Old Tarwater had lived under his roof, been
so conscious of the old man's presence.

Once the boy had stopped suddenly in front of a
tall building and had stood glaring up at it with a
peculiar ravaged look of recognition. Puzzled, Rayber
said, "You look as if you've been here before."

"I lost my hat there," he muttered.

"Your hat is on your head," Rayber said. He could not look at the object without irritation. He wished to God there were some way to get it off him.

"My first hat," the boy said. "It fell," and he had rushed on, away from the place as if he could not stand to be near it.

Only one other time had he shown a particular interest. He had stopped with a kind of lurch backwards in front of a large grimey garage-like structure with two yellow and blue painted windows in the front of it, and had stood there, precariously balanced as if he were arresting himself in the middle of a fall. Rayber recognized the place for some kind of pentecostal tabernacle. Over the door was a paper banner bearing the words, UNLESS YE BE BORN AGAIN YE SHALL NOT HAVE EVERLASTING LIFE. Beneath it a poster showed a man and woman and child holding hands. "Hear the Carmodys for Christ!" it said. "Thrill to the Music, Message, and Magic of this team!"

Rayber was well enough aware of the boy's trouble to understand the sinister pull such a place would have on his mind. "Does this interest you?" he asked drily. "Does it remind you of something in particular?"

Tarwater was very pale. "Horse manure," he whispered.

Rayber smiled. Then he laughed. "All such people have in life," he said, "is the conviction they'll rise again."

The boy steadied himself, his eyes still on the banner but as if he had reduced it to a small spot a great distance away.

"They won't rise again?" he said. The statement had the lilt of a question and Rayber realized with an intense thrill of pleasure that his opinion, for the first time, was being called for.

"No," he said simply, "they won't rise again." There was a profound finality in his tone. The grimey structure might have been the carcass of a beast he had just brought down. He put his hand experimentally on the boy's shoulder. It was suffered to remain there.

In a voice unsteady with the sudden return of enthusiasm he said, "That's why I want you to learn all you can. I want you to be educated so that you can take your place as an intelligent man in the world. This fall when you start school . . ."

The shoulder was roughly withdrawn and the boy, throwing him one dark look, removed himself to the farthest edge of the sidewalk.

He wore his isolation like a mantle, wrapped it around himself as if it were a garment signifying the elect. Rayber had intended to keep notes on him and write up his most important observations but each night his energy had been too depleted to permit him to do any work. He had dropped off every night into a restless sleep, afraid that he would wake up and find the boy gone. He felt he had hastened his urge to leave by confronting him with the test. He had intended giving him the standard ones, intelligence and aptitude, and then going on to some he had perfected himself dealing with emotional factors. He had thought that in this way he could ferret to the center of the emotional infection. He had laid a simple aptitude test out on the kitchen table—the printed book and a few newly sharpened pencils. "This is a kind of game," he said. "Sit down and see what you can make of it. I'll help you begin."

The expression that came over the boy's face was very peculiar. His eyelids lowered just slightly; his mouth failed a smile by only a fraction; his look was compounded of fury and superiority. "Play with it yourself," he said. "I ain't taking no *test*," and he spit the word out as if it were not fit to pass between his lips.

Rayber sized up the situation. Then he said, "Maybe you don't really know how to read and write. Is that the trouble?"

The boy thrust his head forward. "I'm free," he hissed. "I'm outside your head. I ain't in it. I ain't in it and I ain't about to be."

His uncle laughed. "You don't know what freedom is," he said, "you don't . . ." but the boy turned and strode off.

It was no use. He could no more be reasoned with than a jackal. Nothing gave him pause—except Bishop, and Rayber knew that the reason Bishop gave him pause was because the child reminded him of the old man. Bishop looked like the old man grown backwards to the lowest form of innocence, and Rayber observed that the boy strictly avoided looking him in the eye. Wherever the child happened to be standing or sitting or walking seemed to be for Tarwater a dangerous hole in space that he must keep away from at all costs. Rayber was afraid that Bishop would drive him away with his friendliness. He was always creeping up to touch him and when the boy was aware of his being near, he would draw himself up like a snake ready to strike and hiss, "Git!" and Bishop would scurry off to watch him again from behind the nearest piece of furniture.

The schoolteacher understood this too. Every problem the boy had he had had himself and had conquered, or had for the most part conquered, for he had not conquered the problem of Bishop. He had only learned to live with it and had learned too that he could not live without it.

When he had got rid of his wife, he and the child had begun living together in a quiet automatic fashion like two bachelors whose habits were so smoothly connected that they no longer needed to take notice of each other. In the winter he sent him to a school for exceptional children and he had made great strides. He could wash himself, dress himself, feed himself, go to the toilet by himself and make peanut butter sandwiches though sometimes he put the bread inside. For the most part Rayber lived with him without being painfully aware of his presence but the moments would still come when, rushing from some inexplicable part of himself, he would experience a love for the child so outrageous that he would be left shocked and depressed for days, and trembling for his sanity. It was only a touch of the curse that lay in his blood.

His normal way of looking on Bishop was as an x signifying the general hideousness of fate. He did not believe that he himself was formed in the image and likeness of God but that Bishop was he had no doubt. The little boy was part of a simple equation that required no further solution, except at the moments when with little or no warning he would feel himself overwhelmed by the horrifying love. Anything he looked at too long could bring it on. Bishop did not have to be around. It could be a stick or a stone, the line of a shadow, the absurd old man's walk of a starling crossing the sidewalk. If, without thinking, he lent himself to it, he would feel suddenly a morbid surge of the love that terrified him—powerful enough to throw him to the ground in an act of idiot praise. It was completely irrational and abnormal.

He was not afraid of love in general. He knew the value of it and how it could be used. He had seen it transform in cases where nothing else had worked, such as with his poor sister. None of this had the least bearing on his situation. The love that would overcome him was of a different order entirely. It was not the kind that could be used for the child's improvement or his own. It was love without reason, love for something futureless, love that appeared to exist only to be itself, imperious and all demanding, the kind that would cause him to make a fool of himself in an instant. And it only began with Bishop. It began with Bishop and then like an avalanche covered everything his reason hated. He always felt with it a rush of longing to have the old man's eyes—insane, fish-coloured, violent with their impossible vision of a world transfigured—turned on him once again. The longing was like an undertow in his blood dragging him backwards to what he knew to be madness.

The affliction was in the family. It lay hidden in the line of blood that touched them, flowing from some ancient source, some desert prophet or pole-sitter, until, its power unabated, it appeared in the old man and him and, he surmised, in the boy. Those it touched were condemned to fight it constantly or be ruled by it. The old man had been ruled by it. He, at the cost of a full life, staved it off. What the boy would do hung in the balance.

He had kept it from gaining control over him by what amounted to a rigid ascetic discipline. He did not look at anything too long, he denied his senses unnecessary satisfactions. He slept in a narrow iron bed, worked sitting in a straight-backed chair, ate frugally, spoke little, and cultivated the dullest for friends. At his high school he was the expert on testing. All his professional decisions were prefabricated and did not involve his participation. He was not deceived that this was a whole or a full life, he only knew that it was the way his life had to be lived if it were going to have any dignity at all. He knew that he was the stuff of which fanatics and madmen are made and that he had turned his destiny as if with his bare will. He kept himself upright on a very narrow line between madness and emptiness, and when the time came for him to lose his balance, he intended to lurch toward emptiness and fall on the side of his choice. He recognized that in silent ways he lived an heroic life. The boy would go either his way or old Tarwater's and he was determined to save him for the better course. Although Tarwater claimed to believe nothing the old man had taught him, Rayber could see clearly that there was still a backdrag of belief and fear in him keeping his responses locked.

By virtue of kinship and similarity and experience, Rayber was the person to save him, yet something in the boy's very look drained him, something in his very look, something starved in it, seemed to feed on him. With Tarwater's eyes on him, he felt subjected to a pressure that killed his energy before he had a chance to exert it. The eyes were the eyes of the crazy student father, the personality was the old man's, and somewhere between the two, Rayber's own image was struggling to survive and he was not able to reach it. After three days of walking, he was numb with fatigue and plagued with a sense of his own ineffectiveness. All day his sentences had not quite connected with his thought.

That night they had eaten at an Italian restaurant, dark and not crowded, and he had ordered ravioli for them because Bishop liked it. After each meal the boy removed a piece of paper and a stub of pencil from his pocket and wrote down a figure—his estimate of what the meal was worth. In time he would pay back the total sum, he had said, as he did not intend to be beholden. Rayber would have liked to see the figures and learn what his meals were valued at —the boy never asked the price. He was a finicky eater, pushing the food around on his plate before he ate it and putting each forkful in his mouth as if he suspected it was poisoned. He had pushed the ravioli about, his face drawn. He ate a little of it and then put the fork down.

"Don't you like that?" Rayber had asked. "You can have something else if you don't."

"It all come out the same slop bucket," the boy said.

"Bishop is eating his," Rayber said. Bishop had it smeared all over his face. Occasionally he would feed a spoonful into the sugar bowl or touch the tip of his tongue to the dish.

"That's what I said," Tarwater said, and his glance grazed the top of the child's head, "—a hog might like it."

The schoolteacher put his fork down.

Tarwater was glaring at the dark walls of the room. "He's like a hog," he said. "He eats like a hog and he don't think no more than a hog and when he dies, he'll rot like a hog. Me and you too," he said, looking back at the schoolteacher's mottled face, "will rot like hogs. The only difference between me and you

and a hog is me and you can calculate, but there ain't
any difference between him and one."

Rayber appeared to be gritting his teeth. Finally
he said, "Just forget Bishop exists. You haven't been
asked to have anything to do with him. He's just a
mistake of nature. Try not even to be aware of him."

"He ain't my mistake," the boy muttered. "I ain't
having a thing to do with him."

"Forget him," Rayber said in a short harsh voice.

The boy looked at him oddly as if he were beginning to perceive his secret affliction. What he saw
or thought he saw seemed grimly to amuse him.
"Let's leave out of here," he said, "and get to walking
again."

"We are not going to walk tonight," Rayber said.
"We are going home and go to bed." He said it with
a firmness and finaltiy he had not used before. The
boy had only shrugged.

As Rayber lay watching the window darken, he
felt that all his nerves were stretched through him
like high tension wire. He began trying to relax one
muscle at a time as the books recommended, beginning with those in the back of his neck. He emptied
his mind of everything but the just visible pattern of
the hedge against the screen. Still he was alert for
any sound. Long after he lay in complete darkness,
he was still alert, unrelaxed, ready to spring up at the
least creak of a floor board in the hall. All at once he
sat up, wide awake. A door opened and closed. He
leapt up and ran across the hall into the opposite

room. The boy was gone. He ran back to his own room and pulled his trousers on over his pajamas. Then grabbing his coat, he went out the house by way of the kitchen, barefooted, his jaw set.

V

KEEPING close to his side of the hedge, he crept through the dark damp grass toward the street. The night was close and very still. A light went on in a window of the next house and revealed, at the end of the hedge, the hat. It turned slightly and Rayber saw the sharp profile beneath it, the set thrust of a jaw very like his own. The boy was stopped still, most likely taking his bearings, deciding which direction to walk in.

He turned again and again Rayber saw only the hat, intransigently ground upon his head, fierce-looking even in the dim light. It had the boy's own defiant quality, as if its shape had been formed over the years by his personality. It had been the first thing that Rayber had seen must go. It suddenly moved out of the light and vanished.

Rayber slipped through the hedge and followed, soundless on his bare feet. Nothing cast a shadow. He could barely make out the boy a quarter of a block in front of him, except when occasionally light from a window outlined him briefly. Since Rayber didn't know whether he thought he was leaving for good or only going for a walk on his own, he decided not to shout and stop him but to follow silently and observe. He turned off his hearing aid and pursued the dim figure as if in a dream. The boy walked even faster at night than in the day time and was always on the verge of vanishing.

Rayber felt the accelerated beat of his heart. He took a handkerchief out of his pocket and wiped his forehead and inside the neck of his pajama top. He walked over something sticky on the sidewalk and shifted hurriedly to the other side, cursing under his breath. Tarwater was heading toward town. Rayber thought it likely he was returning to see something that had secretly interested him. He might discover tonight what he would have found by testing if the boy had not been so pig-headed. He felt the insidious pleasure of revenge and checked it.

A patch of sky blanched, revealing for a moment the outlines of the housetops. Tarwater turned suddenly to the right. Rayber cursed himself for not stopping long enough to get his shoes. They had come into a neighborhood of large ramshackle boarding houses with porches that abutted the sidewalks. On some of them late sitters were rocking and watching the street. He felt eyes in the darkness move on him and he turned on the hearing aid again. On one porch a woman rose and leaned over the banister. She stood with her hands on her hips, looking him over, taking in his bare feet, the striped pajama coat under his seersucker suit. Irritated, he glanced back at her. The thrust of her neck indicated a conclusion formed. He buttoned his coat and hurried on.

The boy stopped on the next corner. His lean shadow made by a street light slanted to the side of him. The hat's shadow, like a knob at the top of it, turned to the right and then the left. He appeared to be considering his direction. Rayber's muscles felt suddenly weighted. He was not conscious of his fatigue until the pace slackened.

Tarwater turned to the left and Rayber began angrily to move again. They went down a street of dilapidated stores. When Rayber turned the next corner, the gaudy cave of a movie house yawned to the side of him. A knot of small boys stood in front of it. "Forgot yer shoes!" one of them chirruped. "Forgot yer shirt!"

He began a kind of limping lope.

The chorus followed him down the block. "Hi yo Silverwear, Tonto's lost his underwear! What in the heck do we care?"

He kept his eye wrathfully on Tarwater who was turning to the right. When he reached the corner and turned, he saw the boy stopped in the middle of the block, looking in a store window. He slipped into a narrow entrance a few yards farther on where a flight of steps led upward into darkness. Then he looked out.

Tarwater's face was strangely lit from the window he was standing before. Rayber watched curiously for a few moments. It looked to him like the face of someone starving who sees a meal he can't reach laid out before him. At last, something he *wants,* he thought, and determined that tomorrow he would return and buy it. Tarwater reached out and touched the glass and then drew his hand back slowly. He hung there as if he could not take his eyes off what it was he wanted. A pet shop, perhaps, Rayber thought. Maybe he wants a dog. A dog might make all the difference. Abruptly the boy broke away and moved on.

Rayber stepped out of the entrance and made for the window he had left. He stopped with a shock of disappointment. The place was only a bakery. The window was empty except for a loaf of bread pushed to the side that must have been overlooked when the shelf was cleaned for the night. He stared, puzzled, at the empty window for a second before he started after the boy again. Everything a false alarm, he thought with disgust. If he had eaten his dinner, he wouldn't be hungry. A man and woman strolling past looked with interest at his bare feet. He glared at them, then glanced to the side and saw his bloodless wired reflection in the glass of a shoe shop. The boy disappeared all at once into an alley. My God, Rayber thought, how long is this going on?

He turned into the alley, which was unpaved and so dark that he could not see Tarwater in it at all. He was certain that any minute he would cut his feet on broken glass. A garbage can materialized in his path. There was a noise like the collapse of a tin house and he found himself sitting up with his hand and one foot in something unidentifiable. He scrambled up and limped on, hearing his own curses like the voice of a stranger broadcast through his hearing aid. At the end of the alley, he saw the lean figure in the middle of the next block, and with a sudden fury he began to run.

The boy turned into another alley. Doggedly Rayber ran on. At the end of the second alley, the boy turned to the left. When Rayber reached the street, Tarwater was standing still in the middle of the next block. With a furtive look around him, he vanished, apparently into the building he had been facing. Rayber dashed forward. As he reached the place, singing burst flatly against his eardrums. Two blue and yellow windows glared at him in the darkness like the eyes of some Biblical beast. He stopped in front of the banner and read the mocking words, UNLESS YE BE BORN AGAIN. . . .

That the boy's corruption was this deep did not surprise him. What unstrung him was the thought that what Tarwater carried into the atrocious temple was his own imprisoned image. Enraged, he started around the building to locate a window he could look through and see the boy's face among the crowd. When he saw him, he would roar at him to come out. The windows near the front were all too high but toward the back, he found a lower one. He pushed through a straggly shrub beneath it and, his chin just above the ledge, looked into what appeared to be a small ante-room. A door on the other side of it opened onto a stage and there a man in a bright blue suit was standing in a spotlight, leading a hymn. Rayber could not see into the main body of the building where the people were. He was about to move away when the man brought the hymn to a close and began to speak.

"Friends," he said, "the time has come. The time we've all been waiting for this evening. Jesus said suffer the little children to come unto Him and forbid them not and maybe it was because He knew that it would be the little children that would call others to Him, maybe He knew, friends, maybe He hadda hunch."

Rayber listened angrily, too exhausted to move away once he had stopped.

"Friends," the preacher said, "Lucette has travelled the world over telling people about Jesus. She's been to India and China. She's spoken to all the rulers of the world. Jesus is wonderful, friends. He teaches us wisdom out of the mouths of babes!"

Another child exploited, Rayber thought furiously.

It was the thought of a child's mind warped, of a child led away from reality that always enraged him, bringing back to him his own childhood's seduction. Glaring at the spotlight, he saw the man there as a blur which he looked through, down the length of his life until what confronted him were the old man's fish-coloured eyes. He saw himself taking the offered hand and innocently walking out of his own yard, innocently walking into six or seven years of unreality. Any other child would have thrown off the spell in a week. He could not have. He had analysed his case and closed it. Still, every now and then he would live over the five minutes it had taken his father to snatch him away from Powderhead. Through the blur of the man on the stage, as if he were looking into a transparent nightmare, he had the experience again. He and his uncle sat on the steps of the house at Powderhead watching his father emerge from the woods and sight them across the field. His uncle leaned forward, squinting, his hand cupped over his eyes, and he sat with his hands clenched between his knees, his heart threshing from side to side as his father moved closer and closer.

"Lucette travels with her mother and daddy and I want you to meet them because a mother and daddy have to be unselfish to share their only child with the world," the preacher said. "Here they are, friends—Mr. and Mrs. Carmody!"

While a man and woman moved into the light, Rayber had a clear vision of plowed ground, of the shaded red ridges that separated him from the lean figure approaching. He had let himself imagine that the field had an undertow that would drag his father backwards and suck him under, but he came on inexorably, only stopping every now and then to put a finger in his shoe and push out a clod of dirt.

"He's going to take me back with him," he said.

"Back with him where?" his uncle growled. "He ain't got any place to take you back to."

"He can't take me back with him?"

"Not where you were before."

"He can't take me back to town?"

"I never said nothing about town," his uncle said.

He saw vaguely that the man in the spotlight had sat down but that the woman was still standing. She became a blur and he saw his father again, getting closer and closer and he had one impulse to dart up and run through his uncle's house and tear out the back to the woods. He would have raced along the path, familiar to him then, and sliding and slipping over the waxy pine needles, he would have run down and down until he reached the thicket of bamboo and would have pushed through it and out onto the other side and would have fallen into the stream and lain there, panting and wheezing and safe where he had been born again, where his head had been thrust by his uncle into the water and brought up again into a new life. Sitting on the step, his leg muscles twitched as if they were ready for him to spring up but he remained absolutely still. He could see the line of his father's mouth, the line that had gone past the point of exasperation, past the point of loud wrath to a kind of stoked rage that would feed him for months.

While the woman evangelist, tall and raw-boned, was speaking of the hardships she had endured, he watched his father as he reached the edge of the yard and stepped onto the packed dirt, his face a slick pink from the exertion of crossing a field. He was drawing short hard breaths. For an instant he seemed about to reach forward and snatch him but he remained where he was. His pale eyes moved carefully over the rock-like figure watching him steadily from the steps, at the red hands knotted on the heavy thighs and then at the gun lying on the porch. He said, "His mother wants him back, Mason. I don't know why. For my part you could have him but you know how she is."

"A drunken whore," his uncle growled.

"Your sister, not mine," his father said, and then said, "All right boy, snap it up," and nodded curtly to him.

He explained in a high reedy voice the exact reason he could not go back, "I've been born again."

"Great," his father said, "great." He took a step forward and grabbed his arm and yanked him to his feet. "Glad you got him fixed up, Mason," he said. "One bath more or less won't hurt the bugger."

He had had no chance to see his uncle's face. His father had already lept into the plowed field and was dragging him across the furrows while the pellets pierced the air over their heads. His shoulders, just under the window ledge, jumped. He shook his head to clear it.

"For ten years I was a missionary in China," the woman was saying, "for five years I was a missionary in Africa, and one year I was a missionary in Rome where minds are still chained in priestly darkness; but for the last six years, my husband and I have travelled the world over with our daughter. They have been years of trial and pain, years of hardship and suffering." She had on a long dramatic cape, one side of which was turned backward over her shoulder to reveal a red lining.

His father's face was suddenly very close to his own. "Back to the real world, boy," he was saying, "back to the real world. And that's me and not him, see? Me and not him," and he heard himself screaming, "It's him! Him! Him and not you! And I've been born again and there's not a thing you can do about it!"

"Christ in hell," his father said, "believe it if you want to. Who cares? You'll find out soon enough."

The woman's tone had changed. The sound of something grasping drew his attention again. "We have not had an easy time. We have been a hard-working team for Christ. People have not always been generous to us. Only here are the people really generous. I am from Texas and my husband is from Tennessee but we have travelled the world over. We know," she said in a deepened softened voice, "where the people are really generous."

Rayber forgot himself and listened. He felt a relief from his pain, recognizing that the woman was only after money. He could hear the beginning click of coins falling in a plate.

"Our little girl began to preach when she was six. We saw that she had a mission, that she had been called. We saw that we could not keep her to ourselves and so we have endured many hardships to give her to the world, to bring her to you tonight. To us," she said, "you are as important as the great rulers of the world!" Here she lifted the end of her cape and holding it out as a magician would made a low bow. After a moment she lifted her head, gazed in front of her as if at some grand vista, and disappeared from view. A little girl hobbled into the spotlight.

Rayber cringed. Simply by the sight of her he could tell that she was not a fraud, that she was only exploited. She was eleven or twelve with a small delicate face and a head of black hair that looked too thick and heavy for a frail child to support. A cape like her mother's was turned back over one shoulder and her skirt was short as if better to reveal the thin legs twisted from the knees. She held her arms over her head for a moment. "I want to tell you people the story of the world," she said in a loud high child's voice. "I want to tell you why Jesus came and what happened to Him. I want to tell you how He'll come again. I want to tell you to be ready. Most of all," she said, "I want to tell you to be ready so that on the last day you'll rise in the glory of the Lord."

Rayber's fury encompassed the parents, the preacher, all the idiots he could not see who were sitting in front of the child, parties to her degradation. She believed it, she was locked tight in it, chained hand and foot, exactly as he had been, exactly as only a child could be. He felt the taste of his own childhood pain laid again on his tongue like a bitter wafer.

"Do you know who Jesus is?" she cried. "Jesus is the Word of God and Jesus is love. The Word of God is love and do you know what love is, you people? If you don't know what love is you won't know Jesus when He comes. You won't be ready. I want to tell you people the story of the world, how it never known when love come, so when love comes again, you'll be ready."

She moved back and forth across the stage, frowning as if she were trying to see the people through the fierce circle of light that followed her. "Listen to me, you people," she said, "God was angry with the world because it always wanted more. It wanted as much as God had and it didn't know what God had but it wanted it and more. It wanted God's own breath, it wanted His very Word and God said, 'I'll make my Word Jesus, I'll give them my Word for a king, I'll give them my very breath for theirs.'

"Listen you people," she said and flung her arms

wide, "God told the world He was going to send it a king and the world waited. The world thought, a golden fleece will do for His bed. Silver and gold and peacock tails, a thousand suns in a peacock's tail will do for His sash. His mother will ride on a four-horned white beast and use the sunset for a cape. She'll trail it behind her over the ground and let the world pull it to pieces, a new one every evening."

To Rayber she was like one of those birds blinded to make it sing more sweetly. Her voice had the tone of a glass bell. His pity encompassed all exploited children—himself when he was a child, Tarwater exploited by the old man, this child exploited by parents, Bishop exploited by the very fact he was alive.

"The world said, 'How long, Lord, do we have to wait for this?' And the Lord said, 'My Word is coming, my Word is coming from the house of David, the king.'" She paused and turned her head to the side, away from the fierce light. Her dark gaze moved slowly until it rested on Rayber's head in the window. He stared back at her. Her eyes remained on his face for a moment. A deep shock went through him. He was certain that the child had looked directly into his heart and seen his pity. He felt that some mysterious connection was established between them.

"'My Word is coming,'" she said, turning back to face the glare, "'my Word is coming from the house of David, the king.'"

She began again in a dirge-like tone. "Jesus came

on cold straw, Jesus was warmed by the breath of an
ox. 'Who is this?' the world said, 'who is this blue-cold
child and this woman, plain as the winter? Is this the
Word of God, this blue-cold child? Is this His will,
this plain winter-woman?'

"Listen you people!" she cried, "the world knew in
its heart, the same as you know in your hearts and I
know in my heart. The world said, 'Love cuts like the
cold wind and the will of God is plain as the winter.
Where is the summer will of God? Where are the
green seasons of God's will? Where is the spring and
summer of God's will?'

"They had to flee into Egypt," she said in a low
voice and turned her head again and this time her
eyes moved directly to Rayber's face in the window
and he knew they sought it. He felt himself caught
up in her look, held there before the judgment seat
of her eyes.

"You and I know," she said turning again, "what
the world hoped then. The world hoped old Herod
would slay the right child, the world hoped old Herod
wouldn't waste those children, but he wasted them.
He didn't get the right one. Jesus grew up and raised
the dead."

Rayber felt his spirit borne aloft. But not those
dead! he cried, not the innocent children, not you,
not me when I was a child, not Bishop, not Frank!
and he had a vision of himself moving like an aveng-
ing angel through the world, gathering up all the children that the Lord, not Herod, had slain.

"Jesus grew up and raised the dead," she cried, "and the world shouted, 'Leave the dead lie. The dead are dead and can stay that way. What do we want with the dead alive?' Oh you people!" she shouted, "they nailed Him to a cross and run a spear through His side and then they said, 'Now we can have some peace, now we can ease our minds.' And they hadn't but only said it when they wanted Him to come again. Their eyes were opened and they saw the glory they had killed.

"Listen world," she cried, flinging up her arms so that the cape flew out behind her, "Jesus is coming again! The mountains are going to lie down like hounds at His feet, the stars are going to perch on His shoulder and when He calls it, the sun is going to fall like a goose for His feast. Will you know the Lord Jesus then? The mountains will know Him and bound forward, the stars will light on His head, the sun will drop down at His feet, but will you know the Lord Jesus then?"

Rayber saw himself fleeing with the child to some enclosed garden where he would teach her the truth, where he would gather all the exploited children of the world and let the sunshine flood their minds.

"If you don't know Him now, you won't know Him then. Listen to me, world, listen to this warning. The Holy Word is in my mouth!

"The Holy Word is in my mouth!" she cried and turned her eyes again on his face in the window. This time there was a lowering concentration in her gaze.

He had drawn her attention entirely away from the congregation.

Come away with me! he silently implored, and I'll teach you the truth, I'll save you, beautiful child!

Her eyes still fixed on him, she cried, "I've seen the Lord in a tree of fire! The Word of God is a burning Word to burn you clean!" She was moving in his direction, the people in front of her forgotten. Rayber's heart began to race. He felt some miraculous communication between them. The child alone in the world was meant to understand him. "Burns the whole world, man and child," she cried, her eye on him, "none can escape." She stopped a little distance from the end of the stage and stood silent, her whole attention directed across the small room to his face on the ledge. Her eyes were large and dark and fierce. He felt that in the space between them, their spirits had broken the bonds of age and ignorance and were mingling in some unheard of knowledge of each other. He was transfixed by the child's silence. Suddenly she raised her arm and pointed toward his face. "Listen you people," she shrieked, "I see a damned soul before my eye! I see a dead man Jesus hasn't raised. His head is in the window but his ear is deaf to the Holy Word!"

Rayber's head, as if it had been struck by an invisible bolt, dropped from the ledge. He crouched on the ground, his furious spectacled eyes glittering behind the shrubbery. Inside she continued to shriek, "Are you deaf to the Lord's Word? The Word of God is a burning Word to burn you clean, burns man and child, man and child the same, you people! Be saved in the Lord's fire or perish in your own! Be saved in . . ."

He was groping fiercely about him, slapping at his coat pockets, his head, his chest, not able to find the switch that would cut off the voice. Then his hand touched the button and he snapped it. A silent dark relief enclosed him like shelter after a tormenting wind. For a while he sat limp behind the bush. Then the reason for his being here returned to him and he experienced a moment of loathing for the boy that earlier would have made him shudder. He wanted nothing but to get back home and sink into his own bed, whether the boy returned or not.

He got out of the shrubbery and started toward the front of the building. As he turned onto the sidewalk, the door of the tabernacle flew open and Tarwater flung himself out. Rayber stopped abruptly.

The boy stood confronting him, his face strangely mobile as if successive layers of shock were settling on it to form a new expression. After a moment he raised his arm in an uncertain gesture of greeting. The sight of Rayber seemed to afford him relief amounting to rescue.

Rayber's face had the wooden look it wore when his hearing aid was off. He did not see the boy's expression at all. His rage obliterated all but the general lines of his figure and he saw them moulded in an irreversible shape of defiance. He grabbed him roughly by the arm and started down the block with him. Both of them walked rapidly as if neither could leave the place fast enough. When they were well down the block, Rayber stopped and swung him around and glared into his face. Through his fury he could not discern that for the first time the boy's eyes were submissive. He snapped on his hearing aid and said fiercely, "I hope you enjoyed the show."

Tarwater's lips moved convulsively. Then he murmured, "I only gone to spit on it."

The schoolteacher continued to glare at him. "I'm not so sure of that."

The boy said nothing. He seemed to have suffered some shock inside the building that had permanently slowed his tongue.

Rayber turned and they walked away in silence. At any point along the way, he could have put his hand on the shoulder next to his and it would not have been withdrawn, but he made no gesture. His head was churning with old rages. The afternoon he had learned the full extent of Bishop's future had sprung to his mind. He saw himself rigidly facing the doctor, a man who had made him think of a bull, impassive, insensitive, his brain already on the next case. He had said, "You should be grateful his health is good. In addition to this, I've seen them born blind as well, some without arms and legs, and one with a heart outside."

He had lurched up, almost ready to strike the man.

"How can I be grateful," he had hissed, "when one—
just one—is born with a heart outside?"

"You'd better try," the doctor had said.

Tarwater walked slightly behind him and Rayber
did not cast a glance back at him. His fury seemed to
be stirring from buried depths that had lain quiet for
years and to be working upward, closer and closer,
toward the slender roots of his peace. When they
reached the house he went in and straight to his bed
without turning to look at the boy's white face which,
drained but expectant, lingered a moment at the
threshold of his door as if waiting for an invitation to
enter.

VI

THE next day, too late, he had the sense of opportunity missed. Tarwater's face had hardened again and the steely gleam in his eye was like the glint of a metal door sealed against an intruder. Rayber felt afflicted with a peculiar chilling clarity of mind in which he saw himself divided in two—a violent and a rational self. The violent self inclined him to see the boy as an enemy and he knew that nothing would hinder his progress with the case so much as giving in to such an inclination. He had waked up after a wild dream in which he chased Tarwater through an interminable alley that twisted suddenly back on itself and reversed the roles of pursuer and pursued. The boy had overtaken him, given him a thunderous blow on the head, and then disappeared. And with his disappearance there had come such an overwhelming feeling of release that Rayber had waked up with a pleasant anticipation that his guest would be gone. He was at once ashamed of the feeling. He settled on a rational, tiring plan for the day and by ten o'clock the three of them were on their way to the natural history museum. He intended to stretch the boy's mind by introducing him to his ancestor, the fish, and to all the great wastes of unexplored time.

They passed part of the territory they had walked over the night before but nothing was said about that trip. Except for the circles under Rayber's eyes, there was nothing about either of them to indicate it had been made. Bishop stumped along, squatting every now and then to pick up something off the sidewalk, while Tarwater, to avoid contamination with them, walked a good four feet to the other side and slightly in advance. I must have infinite patience, I must have infinite patience, Rayber kept repeating to himself.

The museum lay on the other side of the city park which they had not crossed before. As they approached it, the boy paled as if he were shocked to find a wood in the middle of the city. Once inside the park, he stopped and stood glaring about him at the huge trees whose ancient rustling branches intermingled overhead. Patches of light sifting through them spattered the concrete walks with sunshine. Rayber observed that something disturbed him. Then he realized that the place reminded him of Powderhead.

"Let's sit down," he said, wanting both to rest and to observe the boy's agitation. He sat down on a bench and stretched his legs in front of him. He suffered Bishop to climb into his lap. The child's shoelaces were untied and he tied them, for the moment ignoring the boy who was standing there, his face furiously impatient. When he finished tying the shoes, he continued to hold the child, sprawled and grinning, in his lap. The little boy's white head fitted under his chin. Above it Rayber looked at nothing in particular. Then he closed his eyes and in the isolating darkness, he forgot Tarwater's presence. Without warning his hated love gripped him and held him in a vise. He should have known better than to let the child onto his lap.

His forehead became beady with sweat; he looked as if he might have been nailed to the bench. He knew that if he could once conquer this pain, face it and with a supreme effort of his will refuse to feel it, he would be a free man. He held Bishop rigidly. Although the child started the pain, he also limited it, contained it. He had learned this one terrible afternoon when he had tried to drown him.

He had taken him to the beach, two hundred miles away, intending to effect the accident as quickly as possible and return bereaved. It had been a beautiful calm day in May. The beach, almost empty, had stretched down into the gradual swell of ocean. There was nothing to be seen but an expanse of sea and sky and sand and an occasional figure, stick-like, in the distance. He had taken him out on his shoulders and when he was chest deep in the water, had lifted him off, swung the delighted child high in the air and then plunged him swiftly below the surface on his back and held him there, not looking down at what he was doing but up, at an impeturbable witnessing sky, not quite blue, not quite white.

A fierce surging pressure had begun upward beneath his hands and grimly he had exerted more and more force downward. In a second, he felt he was trying to hold a giant under. Astonished, he let himself look. The face under the water was wrathfully contorted, twisted by some primeval rage to save itself. Automatically he released his pressure. Then when he realized what he had done, he pushed down again angrily with all his force until the struggle ceased under his hands. He stood sweating in the water, his own mouth as slack as the child's had been. The body, caught by an undertow, almost got away from him but he managed to come to himself and snatch it. Then as he looked at it, he had a moment of complete terror in which he envisioned his life without the child. He began to shout frantically. He plowed his way out of the water with the limp body. The beach which he had thought empty before had become peopled with strangers converging on him from all directions. A bald-headed man in red and blue Roman striped shorts began at once to administer artificial respiration. Three wailing women and a photographer appeared. The next day there had been a picture in the paper, showing the rescuer, striped bottom forward, working over the child. Rayber was beside him on his knees, watching with an agonized expression. The caption said, OVERJOYED FATHER SEES SON REVIVED.

The boy's voice broke in on him harshly. "All you got to do is nurse an idiot!"

The schoolteacher opened his eyes. They were bloodshot and vague. He might have been returning to consciousness after a blow on the head.

Tarwater was glaring to the side of him. "Come on if you're coming," he said, "and if you ain't, I'm going on about my bidnis."

Rayber didn't answer.

"So long," Tarwater said.

"And where would your business be?" Rayber asked sourly. "At another tabernacle?"

The boy reddened. He opened his mouth and said nothing.

"I nurse an idiot that you're afraid to look at," Rayber said. "Look him in the eye."

Tarwater shot a glance at the top of Bishop's head and left it there an instant like a finger on a candle flame. "I'd as soon be afraid to look at a dog," he said and turned his back. After a moment, as if he were continuing the same conversation, he muttered, "I'd as soon baptize a dog as him. It would be as much use."

"Who said anything about baptizing anybody?" Rayber said. "Is that one of your fixations? Have you taken that bug up from the old man?"

The boy whirled around and faced him. "I told you I only gone there to spit on it," he said tensely. "I ain't going to tell you again."

Rayber watched him without saying anything. He felt that his own sour words had helped him recover himself. He pushed Bishop off and stood up. "Let's get going," he said. He had no intention of discussing it further, but as they moved on silently, he thought better of it.

"Listen Frank," he said, "I'll grant that you went to spit on it. I've never for a second doubted your intelligence. Everything you've done, your very presence here proves that you're above your background, that you've broken through the ceiling the old man set for you. After all, you escaped from Powderhead. You had the courage to attend to him the quickest way and then get out of there. And once out, you came directly to the right place."

The boy reached up and picked a leaf from a tree branch and bit it. A wry expression spread over his face. He rolled the leaf into a ball and threw it away. Rayber continued to speak, his voice detached, as if he had no particular interest in the matter, and his were merely the voice of truth, as impersonal as air.

"Say that you went to spit on it," he said, "the point

is this: there's no need to spit on it. It's not worth spitting on. It's not that important. You've somehow enlarged the significance of it in your mind. The old man used to enrage me until I learned better. He wasn't worth my hate and he's not worth yours. He's only worth our pity." He wondered if the boy were capable of the steadiness of pity. "You want to avoid extremes. They are for violent people and you don't want . . ." —he broke off abruptly as Bishop let loose his hand and galloped away.

They had come out into the center of the park, a concrete circle with a fountain in the middle of it. Water rushed from the mouth of a stone lion's head into a shallow pool and the little boy was flying toward it, his arms flailing like a windmill. In a second he was over the side and in. "Too late, goddammit," Rayber muttered, "he's in." He glanced at Tarwater.

The boy stood arrested in the middle of a step. His eyes were on the child in the pool but they burned as if he beheld some terrible compelling vision. The sun shone brightly on Bishop's white head and the little boy stood there with a look of attention. Tarwater began to move toward him.

He seemed to be drawn toward the child in the water but to be pulling back, exerting an almost equal pressure away from what attracted him. Rayber watched, puzzled and suspicious, moving along with him but somewhat to the side. As he drew closer to the pool, the skin on the boy's face appeared to stretch tighter and tighter. Rayber had the sense that he was moving blindly, that where Bishop was he saw only a spot of light. He felt that something was being enacted before him and that if he could understand it, he would have the key to the boy's future. His muscles were tensed and he was prepared somehow to act. Suddenly his sense of danger was so great that he cried out. In an instant of illumination he understood. Tarwater was moving toward Bishop to baptize him. Already he had reached the edge of the pool. Rayber sprang and snatched the child out of the water and set him down, howling, on the concrete.

His heart was beating furiously. He felt that he had just saved the boy from committing some enormous indignity. He saw it all now. The old man *had* transferred his fixation to the boy, *had* left him with the notion that he must baptize Bishop or suffer some terrible consequence. Tarwater put his foot down on the marble edge of the pool. He leaned forward, his elbow on his knee, looking over the side at his broken reflection in the water. His lips moved as if he were speaking silently to the face forming in the pool. Rayber said nothing. He realized now the magnitude of the boy's affliction. He knew that there was no way to appeal to him with reason. There was no hope of discussing it sanely with him, for it was a compulsion. He saw no way of curing him except perhaps through some shock, some sudden concrete confrontation with the futility, the ridiculous absurdity of performing the empty rite.

He squatted down and began to take off Bishop's

wet shoes. The child had stopped howling and was crying quietly, his face red and hideously distorted. Rayber turned his eyes away.

Tarwater was walking off. He was past the pool, his back strangely bent as if he were being driven away with a whip. He was moving off onto one of the narrow tree-shaded paths.

"Wait!" Rayber shouted. "We can't go to the museum now. We'll have to go home and change Bishop's shoes."

Tarwater could not have failed to hear but he kept on walking and in a second was lost to view.

Goddam backwoods imbecile, Rayber said under his breath. He stood looking at the path where the boy had disappeared. He felt no urge to go after him for he knew that he would be back, that he was held by Bishop. His feeling of oppression was caused now by the certain knowledge that there was no way to get rid of him. He would be with them until he had either accomplished what he came for, or until he was cured. The words the old man had scrawled on the back of the journal rose before him: THE PROPHET I RAISE UP OUT OF THIS BOY WILL BURN YOUR EYES CLEAN. The sentence was like a challenge renewed. I will cure him, he said grimly. I will cure him or know the reason why.

VII

THE Cherokee Lodge was a two-story converted warehouse, the lower part painted white and the upper green. One end sat on land and the other was set on stilts in a glassy little lake across which were dense woods, green and black farther toward the skyline, grey-blue. The long front side of the building, plastered with beer and cigaret signs, faced the highway, which ran about thirty feet away across a dirt road and beyond a narrow stretch of iron weed. Rayber had passed the place before but had never been tempted to stop.

He had selected it because it was only thirty miles from Powderhead and because it was cheap and he arrived there the next day with the two boys in time for them to take a walk and look around before they ate. The ride up had been oppressively silent, the boy sitting as usual on his side of the car like some foreign dignitary who would not admit speaking the language—the filthy hat, the stinking overalls, worn defiantly like a national costume.

Rayber had hit upon his plan in the night. It was to take him back to Powderhead and make him face what he had done. What he hoped was that if seeing and feeling the place again were a real shock, the boy's trauma might suddenly be revealed. His irrational fears and impulses would burst out and his uncle—sympathetic, knowing, uniquely able to understand—would be there to explain them to him. He had not said they were going to Powderhead. So far as the boy knew, this was to be a fishing trip. He thought that an afternoon of relaxation in a boat before the experiment would help ease the tension, his own as well as Tarwater's.

On the drive up, his thoughts had been interrupted once when he saw Bishop's face rise unorganized into the rearview mirror and then disappear as he attempted to crawl over the top of the front seat and climb into Tarwater's lap. The boy had turned and without looking at him had given the panting child a firm push onto the back seat again. One of Rayber's immediate goals was to make him understand that his urge to baptize the child was a kind of *sickness* and that a sign of returning health would be his ability to begin looking Bishop in the eye. Rayber felt that once he could look the child in the eye, he would have confidence in his ability to resist the morbid impulse to baptize him.

When they got out of the car, he watched the boy closely, trying to discover his first reaction to being in the country again. Tarwater stood for a moment, his head lifted sharply as if he detected some familiar odor moving from the pine forest across the lake. His long face, depending from the bulb-shaped hat, made Rayber think of a root jerked suddenly out of the ground and exposed to the light. The boy's eyes narrowed so that the lake must have been reduced to the width of a knife-blade in his sight. He looked at the water with a peculiar undisguised hostility. Rayber even thought that as his eye fell on it, he began to tremble. At least he was certain that his hands clenched. His glare steadied, then with his usual precipitous gait, he set off around the building without looking back.

Bishop climbed out of the car and thrust his face against his father's side. Absently Rayber put his hand on the little boy's ear and rubbed it gingerly, his fingers tingling as if they touched the sensitive scar of some old wound. Then he pushed the child aside, picked up the bag and started toward the screen door of the lodge. As he reached it, Tarwater came quickly around the side of the building with the distinct look to Rayber of being pursued. His feeling for the boy alternated drastically between compassion for his haunted look and fury at the way he was treated by him. Tarwater acted as if to see him at all required a special effort. Rayber opened the screen door and stepped inside, leaving the two boys to come in or not as they pleased.

The interior was dark. To the left he made out a reception desk with a heavy plain-looking woman behind it, leaning on her elbows. He set the bags down and gave her his name. He had the feeling that though her eyes were on him, they were looking behind him. He glanced around. Bishop was a few feet away, gaping at her.

"What's your name, Sugarpie?" she asked.

"His name is Bishop," Rayber said shortly. He was always irked when the child was stared at.

The woman tilted her head sympathetically. "I reckon you're taking him off to give his mother a little rest," she said, her eyes full of curiosity and compassion.

"I have him all the time," he said and added before he could stop himself, "his mother abandoned him."

"No!" she breathed. "Well," she said, "it takes all kinds of women. I couldn't leave a child like that."

You can't even take your eyes off him, he thought irritably and began to fill out the card. "Are the boats for rent?" he asked without looking up.

"Free for the guests," she said, "but anybody gets

drowned, that's their lookout. How about him? Can
he sit still in a boat?"

"Nothing ever happens to him," he murmured, finishing the card and turning it around to her.

She read it, then she glanced up and stared at Tarwater. He was standing a few feet behind Bishop,
looking around him suspiciously, his hands in his
pockets and his hat pulled down. She began to scowl.
"That boy there—is yours too?" she asked, pointing
the pen at him as if this were inconceivable.

Rayber realized that she must think he was some
one hired for a guide. "Certainly, he's mine too," he
said quickly and in a voice the boy could not fail to
hear. He made it a point to impress on him that he
was wanted, whether he cared to be wanted or not.

Tarwater lifted his head and returned the woman's
stare. Then he took a stride forward and thrust his
face at her. "What do you mean—is his?" he demanded.

"Is his," she said, drawing back. "You don't look it
is all." Then she frowned as if, continuing to study
him, she began to see a likeness.

"And I ain't it," he said. He snatched the card from
her and read it. Rayber had written, "George F. Rayber, Frank and Bishop Rayber," and their address.
The boy put the card down on the desk and picked
up the pen, gripping it so hard that his fingers turned
red at the tips. He crossed out the name *Frank* and
underneath in an old man's meticulous hand he began to write something else.

Rayber looked at the woman helplessly and lifted his shoulders as if to say, "I have more than one problem," and shrug it off, but the gesture ended in a violent tremor. To his horror he felt the side of his mouth give a series of quick jerks. He had an instant's premonition that if he wished to save himself, he should leave at once, that the trip was doomed.

The woman handed him the key and, looking at him suspiciously, said, "Up the steps yonder and four doors down to the right. We don't have anybody to tote the bags."

He took the key and started up a rickety flight of steps to the left. Halfway up, he paused and said in a voice in which there was a remnant of authority, "Bring up that bag when you come, Frank."

The boy was finishing his essay on the card and gave no indication of hearing.

The woman's curious gaze followed Rayber up the stairs until he disappeared. She observed as his feet passed the level of her head that he had on one brown sock and one grey. His shoes were not run-down but he might have slept in his seersucker suit every night. He was in bad need of a haircut and his eyes had a peculiar look—like something human trapped in a switch box. Has come here to have a nervous breakdown, she said to herself. Then she turned her head. Her eyes rested on the two boys, who had not moved. And who wouldn't? she asked herself.

The afflicted child looked as if he must have dressed himself. He had on a black cowboy hat and a pair of short khaki pants that were too tight even for his narrow hips and a yellow t-shirt that had not been washed any time lately. Both his brown hightop shoes were untied. The upper part of him looked like an old man and the lower part like a child. The other, the mean-looking one, had picked up the desk card again and was reading over what he had written on it. He was so taken up with it that he did not see the little boy reaching out to touch him. The instant the child touched him, the country boy's shoulders leapt. He snatched his touched hand up and jammed it in his pocket. "Leave off!" he said in a high voice. "Git away and quit bothering me!"

"Mind how you talk to one of them there, you boy!" the woman hissed.

He looked at her as if it were the first time she had spoken to him. "Them there what?" he murmured.

"That there kind," she said, looking at him fiercely as if he had profaned the holy.

He looked back at the afflicted child and the woman was startled by the expression on his face. He seemed to see the little boy and nothing else, no air around him, no room, no nothing, as if his gaze had slipped and fallen into the center of the child's eyes and was still falling down and down and down. The little boy turned after a second and skipped off toward the steps and the country boy followed, so directly that he might have been attached to him by a tow-line. The child began to scramble up the steps on his hands and knees, kicking his feet up on each one.

Then suddenly he flipped himself around and sat down squarely in the country boy's way and stuck his feet out in front of him, apparently wanting his shoes tied. The country boy stopped still. He hung over him like some one bewitched, his long arms bent uncertainly.

The woman watched fascinated. He ain't going to tie them, she said, not him.

He leaned over and began to tie them. Frowning furiously, he tied one and then the other and the child watched, completely absorbed in the operation. When the boy finished tying them, he straightened himself and said in a querulous voice, "Now git on and quit bothering me with them laces," and the child flipped over on his hands and feet and scrambled up the stairs, making a great din.

Confused by this kindness, the woman called, "Hey boy."

She had intended to say, "Whose boy are you?" but she said nothing, her mouth opening on a vanished sentence. His eyes as they turned and looked down at her were the color of the lake just before dark when the last daylight has faded and the moon has not risen yet, and for an instant she thought she saw something fleeing across the surface of them, a lost light that came from nowhere and vanished into nothing. For some moments they stared at each other without issue. Finally, convinced she had not seen it, she muttered, "Whatever devil's work you mean to do, don't do it here."

He continued to look down at her. "You can't just say NO," he said. "You got to do NO. You got to show it. You got to show you mean it by doing it. You got to show you're not going to do one thing by doing another. You got to make an end of it. One way or another."

"Don't you do nothing here," she said, wondering what he would do here.

"I never ast to come here," he said. "I never ast for that lake to be set down in front of me," and he turned and moved on up the stairs.

The woman looked in front of her for some time as if she were seeing her own thoughts before her like unintelligible handwriting on the wall. Then she looked down at the card on the counter and turned it over. "Francis Marion Tarwater," he had written. "Powderhead, Tennessee. NOT HIS SON."

VIII

AFTER they had had their lunch, the schoolteacher suggested they get a boat and fish awhile. Tarwater could tell that he was watching him again, his little eyes protected and precise behind his glasses. He had been watching him ever since he came but now he was watching in a different way: he was watching for something that he planned to make happen. The trip was designed to be a trap but the boy had no attention to spare for it. His mind was entirely occupied with saving himself from the larger grander trap that he felt set all about him. Ever since his first night in the city when he had seen once and for all that the schoolteacher was of no significance—nothing but a piece of bait, an insult to his intelligence—his mind had been engaged in a continual struggle with the silence that confronted him, that demanded he baptize the child and begin at once the life the old man had prepared him for.

It was a strange waiting silence. It seemed to lie all around him like an invisible country whose borders he was always on the edge of, always in danger of crossing. From time to time as they had walked in the city, he had looked to the side and seen his own form alongside him in a store window, transparent as a snakeskin. It moved beside him like some violent ghost who had already crossed over and was reproaching him from the other side. If he turned his head the opposite way, there would be the dim-witted boy, hanging onto the schoolteacher's coat, watching him. His mouth hung in a lopsided smile but there was a judging sternness about his forehead. The boy never looked lower than the top of his head except by accident for the silent country appeared to be reflected again in the center of his eyes. It stretched out there, limitless and clear.

Tarwater could have baptized him any one of a hundred times without so much as touching him. Each time the temptation came, he would feel that the silence was about to surround him and he was going to be lost in it forever. He would have fallen but for the wise voice that sustained him—the stranger who had kept him company while he dug his uncle's grave.

Sensations, his friend—no longer a stranger—said. Feelings. What you want is a sign, a real sign, suitable to a prophet. If you are a prophet, it's only right you should be treated like one. When Jonah dallied, he was cast three days in a belly of darkness and vomited up in the place of his mission. That was a sign; it wasn't no sensation.

It takes all my time to set you straight. Look at you, he said—going to that fancy-house of God, sitting there like an ape letting that girl-child bend your ear. What did you expect to see there? What did you expect to hear? The Lord speaks to prophets personally and He's never spoke to you, never lifted a finger, never dropped a gesture. And as for that strangeness in your gut, that comes from you, not the Lord. When you were a child you had worms. As likely as not you have them again.

The first day in the city he had become conscious of the strangeness in his stomach, a peculiar hunger. The city food only weakened him. He and his great-uncle had eaten well. If the old man had done nothing else for him, he had heaped his plate. Never a morning he had not awakened to the smell of fatback frying. The schoolteacher paid scarce attention to what he put inside him. For breakfast, he poured a bowl of shavings out of a cardboard box; in the middle of the day he made sandwiches out of lightbread;

and at night he took them to a restaurant, a different one every night run by a different color of foreigner so that he would learn, he said, how other nationalities ate. The boy did not care how other nationalities ate. He had always left the restaurants hungry, conscious of an intrusion in his works. Since the breakfast he had finished sitting in the presence of his uncle's corpse, he had not been satisfied by food, and his hunger had become like an insistent silent force inside him, a silence inside akin to the silence outside, as if the grand trap left him barely an inch to move in, barely an inch in which to keep himself inviolate.

His friend was adamant that he refuse to entertain hunger as a sign. He pointed out that the prophets had been fed. Elijah had lain down under a juniper tree to die and had gone to sleep and an angel of the Lord had come and waked him and fed him a hearth-cake, had done it moreover twice, and Elijah had risen and gone about his business, lasting on the two hearth-cakes forty days and nights. Prophets did not languish in hunger but were fed from the Lord's bounty and the signs given them were unmistakable. His friend suggested he demand an unmistakable sign, not a pang of hunger or a reflection of himself in a store window, but an unmistakable sign, clear and suitable—water bursting forth from a rock, for instance, fire sweeping down at his command and destroying some site he would point to, such as the tabernacle he had gone to spit on.

His fourth night in the city, after he had returned from listening to the child preach, he had sat up in the welfare-woman's bed and raising his folded hat as if he were threatening the silence, he had demanded an unmistakable sign of the Lord.

Now we'll see what class of prophet you are, his friend said. We'll see what the Lord has in mind for you.

The next day the schoolteacher had taken them into a park where trees were fenced together in a kind of island that cars were not allowed in. They had only but entered it when he felt a hush in his blood and a stillness in the atmosphere as if the air were being purged for the approach of revelation. He would have turned and run but the schoolteacher parked himself on a bench and pretended to go to sleep with the dimwit in his lap. The trees rustled thickly and the clearing rose to his mind's eye. He imagined the blackened spot in the center of it between the two chimneys, and saw rising from the ashes the burnt-out frames of his own and his uncle's bed. He opened his mouth to get air and the schoolteacher woke up and began asking questions.

He prided himself that from the first night he had answered his questions with the cunning of a Negro, giving no information, knowing nothing, and each time he was questioned, raising his uncle's fury until it was observable under his skin in patches of pink and white. A few of his ready answers and the schoolteacher was willing to move on.

They had walked deeper into the park and he began to feel again the approach of mystery. He would have turned and run in the opposite direction but it was all on him in an instant. The path widened and they were faced with an open space in the middle of the park, a concrete circle with a fountain in the center of it. Water rushed out of the mouth of a stone lion's head into a shallow pool below and as soon as the dim-witted boy saw the water, he gave a whoop and galloped off toward it, flapping his arms like something released from a cage.

Tarwater saw exactly where he was heading, knew exactly what he was going to do.

"Too late, goddamit," the schoolteacher muttered, "he's in."

The child stood grinning in the pool, lifting his feet slowly up and down as if he liked the feel of the wet seeping into his shoes. The sun, which had been tacking from cloud to cloud, emerged above the fountain. A blinding brightness fell on the lion's tangled marble head and gilded the stream of water rushing from his mouth. Then the light, falling more gently, rested like a hand on the child's white head. His face might have been a mirror where the sun had stopped to watch its reflection.

Tarwater started forward. He felt a distinct tension in the quiet. The old man might have been lurking near, holding his breath, waiting for the baptism. His friend was silent as if in the felt presence, he dared not raise his voice. At each step the boy exerted a force backward but he continued nevertheless to move toward the pool. He reached the rim of it and lifted his foot to swing it over the side. Just as his shoe touched the water, the schoolteacher bounded forward and snatched the dimwit out. The child split the silence with his bellow.

Slowly Tarwater's lifted foot came down on the edge of the pool and he leaned there, looking into the water where a wavering face seemed trying to form itself. Gradually it became distinct and still, gaunt and cross-shaped. He observed, deep in its eyes, a look of starvation. I wasn't going to baptize him, he said, flinging the silent words at the silent face. I'd drown him first.

Drown him then, the face appeared to say.

Tarwater stepped back, shocked. Scowling, he straightened himself and moved away. The sun had gone in and there were black caves in the tree branches. Bishop was lying on his back, roaring from a red distorted face, and the schoolteacher stood above him, staring at nothing in particular as if it were he who had received a revelation.

Well, that's your sign, his friend said—the sun coming out from under a cloud and falling on the head of a dimwit. Something that could happen fifty times a day without no one being the wiser. And it took that schoolteacher to save you and just in time. Left to yourself you would already have done it and been lost forever. Listen, he said, you have to quit confusing a madness with a mission. You can't spend your life fooling yourself this way. You have to take hold and put temptation behind you. If you baptize once, you'll be doing it the rest of your life. If it's an idiot this time, the next time it's liable to be a nigger. Save yourself while the hour of salvation is at hand.

But the boy was shaken. He scarcely heard the voice as he walked off deeper into the park and down a path he scarcely saw. When he finally took note of his surroundings, he was sitting on a bench, looking down at his feet where two pigeons were moving in drunken circles. On the other side of the bench was a man of a generally grey appearance who had been examining a hole in his shoe when Tarwater sat down but who stopped then and devoted himself to a close scrutiny of the boy. Finally he reached over and plucked Tarwater's sleeve. The boy looked up into two pale yellow-rimmed eyes.

"Be like me, young fellow," the stranger said, "don't let no jackasses tell you what to do." He was grinning wisely and his eyes held a malevolent promise of unwanted friendship. His voice sounded familiar but his appearance was as unpleasant as a stain.

The boy got up and left hastily. An interesting co-incident, his friend observed, that he should say the same thing as I've been saying. You think there's a trap laid all about you by the Lord. There ain't any trap. There ain't anything except what you've laid for yourself. The Lord is not studying about you, don't know you exist, and wouldn't do a thing about it if He did. You're alone in the world, with only yourself to ask or thank or judge; with only yourself. And me. I'll never desert you.

The first sight that met his eyes when he got out of the car at the Cherokee Lodge was the little lake. It lay there, glass-like, still, reflecting a crown of trees and an infinite overarching sky. It looked so unused that it might only the moment before have been set down by four strapping angels for him to baptize the child in. A weakness working itself up from his knees, reached his stomach and came upward and forced a tremor in his jaw. Steady, his friend said, everywhere you go you'll find water. It wasn't invented yesterday. But remember: water is made for more than one thing. Hasn't the time come? Don't you have to do something at last, one thing to prove you ain't going to do another? Hasn't your hour of dallying passed?

They ate their lunch in the dark other-end of the lobby where the woman who ran the place served meals. Tarwater ate voraciously. With an expression of intense concentration, he ate six buns filled with barbecue and drank three cans of beer. He might have been preparing himself for a long journey or for some action that would take all his strength. Rayber observed his sudden appetite for the poor food and decided that he was eating compulsively. He wondered if the beer might loosen his tongue, but in the boat he was as glum as ever. He sat hunched over, his hat pulled down, and scowled at the spot where his line disappeared in the water.

They had managed to get the boat away from the dock before Bishop came out of the lodge. The woman had drawn him to an icecooler and produced a green popsickle which she held up for him while she gazed fascinated into his mysterious face. They were in the middle of the lake before he came clattering down the dock, the woman running behind. She snatched him just in time to keep him from plunging over the edge.

Rayber made a frantic grabbing motion in the boat and cried out. Then he reddened and scowled. "Don't look," he said, "she'll take care of him. We need a break."

The boy gazed darkly where the accident had been prevented. The child was a black spot in the glare of his vision. The woman turned him around and started leading him back to the lodge. "It wouldn't have been no great loss if he had drowned," he observed.

Rayber had an instant's picture of himself, standing in the ocean, holding the child's limp body in his arms. With a kind of convulsive motion, he cleared his head of the image. Then he saw that Tarwater had observed his discomposure; he was looking at him with a distinct attention, a peculiar prescient look as if he were about to penetrate some secret.

"Nothing ever happens to that kind of child," Rayber said. "In a hundred years people may have learned enough to put them to sleep when they're born."

Something appeared to be working on the boy's

face, struggling there, some war between agreement and outrage.

Rayber's blood burned beneath his skin. He tried to restrain the urge to confess. He leaned forward; his mouth opened and closed and then in a dry voice he said, "Once I tried to drown him," and grinned horribly at the boy.

Tarwater's lips parted as if only they had heard, but he said nothing.

"It was a failure of nerve," Rayber said. The glare on the water gave him the sensation of glancing at white fire each time he looked up or out where it was reflected on the water. He turned down the brim of his hat all the way around.

"You didn't have the guts," Tarwater said as if he would put it in a more accurate way. "He always told me you couldn't do nothing, couldn't act."

The schoolteacher leaned forward and said between his teeth, "I've resisted him. I've done that. What have you done? Maybe you attended to him the quickest way but it takes more than that to go against his will for good. Are you quite sure," he said, "are you quite sure you've overcome him? I doubt it. I think you're chained to him right now. I think you're not going to be free of him without my help. I think you've got problems that you're not capable of solving yourself."

The boy scowled and was silent.

The glare pierced Rayber's eyeballs fiercely. He did not think he could stand an afternoon of this. He felt recklessly compelled to pursue the subject. "How do you like being in the country again?" he growled. "Remind you of Powderhead?"

"I come to fish," the boy said disagreeably.

Goddam you, his uncle thought, all I'm trying to do is save you from being a freak. He was holding his line unbaited in the blinding water. He felt a madness on him to talk about the old man. "I remember the first time I ever saw him," he said. "I was six or seven. I was out in the yard playing and all of a sudden I felt something between me and the sun. Him. I looked up and there he was, those mad fish-coloured eyes looking down at me. Do you know what he said to me—a seven year old child?" He tried to make his voice sound like the old man's. " 'Listen boy,' he said, 'the Lord Jesus Christ sent me to find you. You have to be born again.' " He laughed, glaring at the boy with his furious blistered-looking eyes. "The Lord Jesus Christ had my welfare so at heart that he sent a personal representative. Where was the calamity? The calamity was I believed him. For five or six years. I had nothing else but that. I waited on the Lord Jesus. I thought I'd been born again and that everything was going to be different or was different already because the Lord Jesus had a great interest in me."

Tarwater shifted on the seat. He seemed to listen as if behind a wall.

"It was the eyes that got me," Rayber said. "Children may be attracted to mad eyes. A grown person could have resisted. A child couldn't. Children are cursed with believing."

The boy recognized the sentence. "Some ain't," he said.

The schoolteacher smiled thinly. "And some who think they aren't are," he said, feeling that he was back in control. "It's not as easy as you think to throw it off. Do you know," he said, "that there's a part of your mind that works all the time, that you're not aware of yourself. Things go on in it. All sorts of things you don't know about."

Tarwater looked around him as if he were vainly searching for a way to get out of the boat and walk off.

"I think you're basically very bright," his uncle said. "I think you can understand the things that are said to you."

"I never came for no school lesson," the boy said rudely. "I come to fish. I ain't worried what my underhead is doing. I know what I think when I do it and when I get ready to do it, I don't talk no words. I do it." There was a dull anger in his voice. He was becoming aware of how much he had eaten. The food appeared to be sinking like a leaden column inside him and to be pushed back at the same time by the hunger it had intruded upon.

The schoolteacher watched him a moment and then said, "Well anyway, as far as the baptizing went, the old man could have spared himself. I was already baptized. My mother never overcame her upbringing and she had had it done. But the damage to me of having it done at the age of seven was tremendous. It made a lasting scar."

The boy looked up suddenly as if there had been a tug at his line. "Him back there," he said and jerked his head toward the lodge, "he ain't been baptized?"

"No," Rayber said. He looked at him narrowly. He thought that if he could get the right words in now, he might do some good, might give him a painless lesson. "I may not have the guts to drown him," he said, "but I have the guts to maintain my self-respect and not to perform futile rites over him. I have the guts not to become the prey of superstitions. He is what he is and there's nothing for him to be born into. My guts," he finished, "are in my head."

The boy only stared at him, his eyes filmed with a dull cast of nausea.

"The great dignity of man," his uncle said, "is his ability to say: I am born once and no more. What I can see and do for myself and my fellowman in this life is all of my portion and I'm content with it. It's enough to be a man." There was a light ring in his voice. He watched the boy closely to see if he had struck a chord.

Tarwater turned an expressionless face toward the rim of trees that made a paling around the lake. He appeared to stare into emptiness.

Rayber subsided again but he could stand it only a

few minutes. He finished the cigaret and lit another. Then he decided to start off on a new tack and leave the morbid alone for a while. "I'll tell you what I've planned for us to do in a couple of weeks," he said in an almost affable tone. "We're going up for a plane ride. How about that?" He had been considering this, holding it in reserve, thinking it would be the greatest marvel he could produce, something that would surely stir the glum child out of himself.

There was no response. The boy's eyes looked glazed.

"Flying is the greatest engineering achievement of man," Rayber said in an irked voice. "Doesn't it stir your imagination even slightly? If it doesn't I'm afraid there's something wrong with you."

"I done flew," Tarwater said and suppressed a belch. He was entirely occupied with his nausea which he could feel minutely rising.

"How could you have flown?" his uncle asked angrily.

"Him and me give a dollar to go up in one at a fair once," he said. "The houses weren't nothing but matchboxes and the people were invisible—like germs. I wouldn't give you nothing for no airplane. A buzzard can fly."

The schoolteacher gripped both sides of the boat and pushed forward. "He's warped your whole life," he said hoarsely. "You're going to grow up to be a freak if you don't let yourself be helped. You still believe all that crap he taught you. You're eaten up with false guilt. I can read you like a book!" The words were out before he could stop them.

The boy did not even look at him. He leaned over the side of the boat and shuddered. The column, released, formed a sweetly sour circle on the water. A wave of dizziness came over him and then his head cleared. A ravenous emptiness raged in his stomach as if it had reestablished its rightful tenure. He washed his mouth out with a handful of the lake and then wiped his face on his sleeve.

Rayber trembled at his recklessness. He felt certain he had produced this by the word *guilt*. He put his hand on the boy's knee and said, "You'll feel better now."

Tarwater said nothing, glaring with his red-lidded wet eyes at the water as if he were glad he had polluted it.

"It's just as much relief," his uncle said, pressing his advantage, "to get something off your mind as off your stomach. When you tell somebody else your troubles, then they don't bother you so much, they don't get in your blood and make you sick. Somebody else shares the weight. God boy," he said, "you need help. You need to be saved right here now from the old man and everything he stands for. And I'm the one who can save you." With his hat turned down all around he looked like a fanatical country preacher. His eyes glistened. "I know what your problem is," he said. "I know and I can help you. Something's eating you on the inside and I can tell you what it is."

The boy looked at him fiercely. "Why don't you shut your big mouth?" he said. "Why don't you pull that plug out of your ear and turn yourself off? I come to fish. I never came to have no traffic with you."

His uncle snapped the cigaret out of his fingers and it hit the water with a hiss. "Every day," he said coldly, "you remind me more of the old man. You're just like him. You have his future before you."

The boy put down his line. With rigid deliberate movements he lifted his right foot and pulled off his shoe, then his left foot and pulled off that shoe. Then he jerked the straps of his overalls off his shoulders and pulled them down, over his bottom and off. He had on a pair of long thin old man's drawers. He pulled his hat tight down on his head so that it would not possibly come off, then he threw himself out of the boat and swam away, smashing the glassy lake with his cupped fists as if he would like to make it sting and bleed.

My God! Rayber thought, I touched a nerve that time! He kept his eye on the hat in the receding spasm of water. The empty overalls lay at his feet. He grabbed them and felt in the pockets. He took out two stones, a nickel, a box of wooden matches and three nails. He had brought along the new suit and shirt and laid them out on a chair.

Tarwater reached the dock and climbed onto it, the drawers clinging to him, the hat still ground down on his forehead. He turned just in time to see his uncle thrust the bundled overalls below the surface of the water.

Rayber felt as if he had just run across a mined field. At once he was afraid he had made a mistake. The thin rigid figure on the dock did not move. It seemed no more than a wraith-like column of fragile white-hot rage, materialized for an instant, the makings of some pure unfathomable passion. The boy turned and started rapidly toward the lodge and Rayber decided it would be best to linger on the lake a while.

When he came in, he was startled to see Tarwater lying on the far cot in his new clothes and to see Bishop sitting on the other end of it, watching him as if he were mesmerized by the steel-like glint that came from the boy's eyes and was directed into his own. In the plaid shirt and new blue trousers, he looked like a changeling, half his old self and half his new, already half the boy he would be when he was rehabilitated.

Rayber's spirits rose cautiously. He was holding the shoes with the contents of the overall pockets in them. He set them down on the bed and said, "No hard feelings about the clothes, old man. That was just my round."

There was a strange suppressed excitement about

the boy's whole figure, as if he had settled on an inevitable course of action. He did not get up, did not
acknowledge the shoes, but he acknowledged his
uncle's presence by shifting the glint in his eyes
slightly, on him and then away. The schoolteacher
might have been just enough present to be ignored.
Then he looked back at Bishop, triumphantly, boldly,
into the very center of his eyes.

Rayber stood puzzled in the doorway. "Who wants
to go for a ride?" he asked.

Bishop jumped off the bed and was at his side in
an instant. Tarwater started at the little boy's abrupt
disappearance from his field of vision, but he did not
get up or turn his face toward the schoolteacher in
the door.

"Well, we'll leave Frank to his meditations," Rayber said and swung the child around by the shoulder
and left with him, hastily. He wanted to escape before the boy changed his mind.

IX

THE heat was not as intense on the road as it had
been on the lake and he drove with a sense of refresh-
ment he had not felt in the five days Tarwater had
been with him. Once out of sight of the boy, he felt a
pressure had been lifted from the atmosphere. He
eliminated the oppressive presence from his thoughts
and retained only those aspects of it that could be ab-
stracted, clean, into the future person he envisioned.

The sky was a cloudless even blue and he drove
without destination, though he meant before they returned to the lodge to stop and have the car filled for
tomorrow's trip to Powderhead. Bishop was hanging

out the window, his mouth open, letting the air dry his tongue. Automatically, Rayber reached over and locked the door and pulled him back in by his shirt. The child sat, solemnly taking his hat off his head and putting it on his feet, then taking it off his feet and putting it on his head. After he had done this a while, he climbed over the seat and disappeared into the back of the car.

Rayber continued to think of Tarwater's future, his thoughts rewarding except when every now and then the boy's actual face would lodge in the path of a plan. The sudden intrusion of the face made him think of his wife. He seldom thought of her anymore. She would not divorce him for fear she would be given custody of the child and she was now as far away as she could get, in Japan, in some welfare capacity. He was aware of his good fortune in getting rid of her. It was she who had prevented his going back and getting Tarwater away from the old man. She would have been glad enough to have had him if she had not seen him that day when they went to Powderhead to face the old man down. The baby had crawled into the door behind old Tarwater and had sat there, unblinking, as the old man raised his gun and shot Rayber in the leg and then in the ear. She had seen him; Rayber had not; but she would not forget the face. It was not simply that the child was dirty, thin, and grey; it was that its expression had no more changed when the gun went off than the old man's had. This had affected her deeply.

If there had not been something repellent in its face, she said, her maternal instinct would have made her rush forward and snatch it. She had even had that in mind before they arrived and she would have had the courage to do it in spite of the old man's gun; but the child's look had frozen her. It was the opposite of everything appealing. She could not express her exact revulsion, for her feeling was not logical. It had, she said, the look of an adult, not of a child, and of an adult with immovable insane convictions. Its face was like the face she had seen in some medieval paintings where the martyr's limbs are being sawed off and his expression says he is being deprived of nothing essential. She had had the sense, seeing the child in the door, that if it had known that at that moment all its future advantages were being stolen from it, its expression would not have altered a jot. The face for her had expressed the depth of human perversity, the deadly sin of rejecting defiantly one's own obvious good. He had thought all this was possibly her imagination but he understood now that it was not imagination but fact. She said she could not have lived with such a face; she would have been bound to destroy the arrogant look on it.

He reflected wryly that she had not been able to live with Bishop's face any better though there was no arrogance on it. The little boy had climbed up from the floor of the back seat and was hanging over breathing into his ear. By temperament and training she was ready to handle an exceptional child, but not one as exceptional as Bishop, not one bearing her own family name and the face of "that horrible old man." She had returned once in the last two years and demanded that he put Bishop in an institution because she said he could not adequately care for him—though it was plain from the look of him that he thrived like an air plant. His own behaviour on that occasion was still a source of satisfaction to him. He had knocked her not quite halfway across the room.

He had known by that time that his own stability depended on the little boy's presence. He could control his terrifying love as long as it had its focus in Bishop, but if anything happened to the child, he would have to face it in itself. Then the whole world would become his idiot child. He had thought what he would have to do if anything happened to Bishop. He would have with one supreme effort to resist the recognition; with every nerve and muscle and thought, he would have to resist feeling anything at all, thinking anything at all. He would have to anesthetize his life. He shook his head to clear it of these unpleasant thoughts. After it had cleared, they returned one by one. He felt a sinister pull on his consciousness, the familiar undertow of expectation, as if he were still a child waiting on Christ.

The car apparently of its own volition had turned onto a dirt road which without warning pierced his abstraction with its familiarity. He put on his brakes.

It was a narrow corrugated road sunk between

deep red embankments. He looked about him angrily. He had not had the least intention of coming
here today. His car was on the crest of a hill and the
embankments on either side had the look of forming
an entrance to a region he would enter at his peril.
The road sloped down a quarter of a mile or so within
his sight and then turned to disappear behind an
edge of the wood. When he had been on this road
the first time, he had ridden it backwards. A Negro
with a mule and wagon had met him and his uncle at
the junction and they had ridden, their feet dangling
from the back of the wagon. He had leaned over
most of the way, watching the mule's hoofprints in
the dust as they rolled over them.

He decided finally that there would be wisdom in
looking at the place today so that there would be no
surprises for him when he returned tomorrow with
the boy, but for some few moments, he did not move
on. The road that lay in front of him he remembered
as being four or five miles long. Then there was a
stretch through the woods that would have to be
walked and then the field to be crossed. He thought
with distaste of crossing it twice, today and again tomorrow. He thought with distaste of crossing it at
all. Then as if to stop his thinking, he put his foot
down hard on the accelerator and took the road defiantly. Bishop jumped up and down, squealing and
making unintelligible noises of delight.

The road grew narrower as it approached its end
and presently he found himself going over what was

no more than a rutted wagon path, his speed reduced to nothing. He stopped the car finally in a little clearing grown up in Johnson grass and blackberry bushes where what was left of the road touched the edge of the wood. Bishop jumped out and made for the blackberry bushes, attracted by the wasps that buzzed over them. Rayber leapt out and grabbed him just before he reached for one. Gingerly he picked the child a blackberry and handed it to him. The little boy studied it and then, with his fallen smile, returned it to him as if they were performing a ceremony. Rayber flung it away and turned to find the trail through the woods.

He took the child by the hand and pulled him along on what he thought might shortly become a path. The forest rose about him, mysterious and alien. Descending to speak with the shade of my uncle, he thought irritably and wondered if the old man's charred bones would be lying in the ashes. At the thought he almost stopped but did not. Bishop could barely walk for gaping. He lifted his face to stare open-mouthed above him as if he were in some vast overwhelming edifice. His hat fell off and Rayber picked it up and clamped it on his head again and pulled him on. Somewhere below them out of the silence a bird sounded four crystal notes. The child stopped, his breath held.

Rayber knew suddenly that alone with Bishop he could not go to the bottom and cross the field. Tomorrow with the other boy, with his brain engaged, he would be able to make it. He remembered that somewhere along here there was a point where one could look out btween two trees and see the clearing below. When he had first walked through the wood with his uncle, they had stopped at that place and his uncle had pointed down to where, far across the field, a sagging unpainted house stood in a bare hard-packed yard. "Yonder it is," he had said, "and someday it'll be yours—these woods and that field and that fine house." He remembered that his heart had expanded unbelievably.

Suddenly he realized that the place *was* his. In the stress of having the boy return to him, he had never considered the property. He stopped, astounded by the fact that he owned all of this. His trees stood rising above him, majestic and aloof, as if they belonged to an order that had never budged from its first allegiance in the days of creation. His heart began to beat frenetically. Quickly he reduced the whole wood in probable board feet into a college education for the boy. His spirits lifted. He pulled the child along, intending to find the opening where the house could be seen. A few yards below, a sudden patch of sky indicated the spot. He let Bishop go and strode toward it.

The forked tree was familiar to him or seemed so. He put his hand on one trunk, leaned forward and looked out. His gaze moved quickly and unseeing across the field and stopped abruptly where the house had been. Two chimneys stood there, separated by a black space of rubble.

He stood expressionless, his heart strangely wrenched. If the bones were lying in the ashes he could not see them from this distance, but a vision of the old man, farther away in time, rose before him. He saw him standing on the edge of the yard, one hand lifted in an astounded greeting, while he stood a little way off in the field, his fists clenched, trying to shout, trying to make his adolescent fury come out in clear sensible words. He had only stood there shrilling, "You're crazy, you're crazy, you're a liar, you have a head full of crap, you belong in a nut house!" and then had turned and run, carrying away nothing but the registered change in the old man's expression, the sudden drop into some mysterious misery, which afterwards he had never been able to get out of his mind. He saw it as he stared at the two denuded chimneys.

He felt a pressure on his hand and glanced down, continuing to see the same expression and barely noting that it was Bishop he was looking at now. The child wanted to be lifted up to see. Absently he picked him up and held him in the fork of the tree and let him look out. The dull face, the empty grey eyes seemed to Rayber to reflect the ravaged scene across the field. The little boy turned his head after a moment and gazed instead at him. A dreaded sense of loss came over him. He knew that he could not remain here an instant longer. He turned with the child and went quickly back through the woods the way he had come.

On the highway again, he drove gripping the wheel, his face tense, his mind turned on the problem of Tarwater as if his own and not only the boy's salvation depended on his solving it. He had ruined his plan by going to Powderhead too soon. He knew he could not go there again, that he would have to find another way. He went over the afternoon's experience in the boat. There, he thought, he had been on the right track. He had simply not gone far enough. He decided that he would put the whole thing verbally before the boy. He would not argue with him but only tell him, tell him in so many plain words that he had a compulsion and what it was. Whether he answered, whether he cooperated, he would have to listen. He could not escape knowing that there was someone who knew exactly what went on inside him and who understood it for the good reason that it was understandable. He would go the whole way this time and tell him everything. The boy should at least know that he had no secrets. Casually while they ate their supper, he would lift the compulsion from his mind, expose it to the light, and let him have a good look at it. What he did about it would be his own affair. All at once this seemed to him extremely simple, the way he should have proceeded in the first place. Only time simplifies, he thought.

He stopped for gas at a pink stucco filling station where pottery and whirligigs were sold. While the car was being filled, he got out and looked for something to take as a peace offering, for he wanted the encounter to be pleasant if possible. His eye roved over a shelf of false hands, imitation buck teeth, boxes of simulated dog dung to put on the rug, wooden plaques with cynical mottos burnt on them. Finally he saw a combination corkscrew-bottleopener that fit in the palm of the hand. He bought it and left.

When they returned to the room, the boy was still lying on the cot, his face set in a deadly calm as if his eyes had not moved since they left. Again Rayber had a vision of the face his wife must have seen and he experienced a moment's revulsion for the boy that made him tremble. Bishop climbed onto the bottom of the cot and Tarwater returned the child's gaze steadily. He seemed unaware that Rayber was in the room.

"I could eat a horse," the schoolteacher said. "Let's go down."

The boy turned his head and regarded him evenly, with no interest but with no hostility. "It's what you'll get," he said, "if you eat here."

Rayber, unamused, pulled out the corkscrew-bottleopener and dropped it negligently on his chest. "That might come in handy sometime," he said and turned and began to wash his hands at the basin.

In the mirror, he saw him pick it up gingerly and look at it. He pushed the corkscrew out of the circle and then meditatively pushed it back. He studied it back and front and held it in the palm of his hand where it fit like a halfdollar. Presently he said in a grudging voice, "I don't have no use for it but I thank you," and put it in his pocket.

He returned his attention to Bishop as if this were its natural place. He lifted himself on one elbow and fixed the child with a narrow look. "Git up, you," he said slowly. He might have been commanding a small animal he was successfully training. His voice was steady but experimental. The hostility in it seemed contained and directed toward some planned goal. The little boy was watching with complete fascination.

"Git up now, like I tol' you to," Tarwater repeated slowly.

The child obediantly climbed down off the bed.

Rayber felt a twinge of ridiculous jealousy. He stood by, his brows working irritably as the boy moved out of the door without a word and Bishop followed him. After a moment he slung his towel into the basin and walked after them.

The lodge was shaking with the stamping of four couples dancing at the other end of the lobby where the woman who ran the place had a nickelodeon. The three of them sat down at the red tin table and Rayber turned off his hearing aid until the racket should stop. He sat glaring around him, disgruntled at this intrusion.

The dancers were about Tarwater's age but they

might have belonged to a different species entirely. The girls could be distinguished from the boys only by their tight skirts and bare legs; their faces and heads were alike. They danced with a furious stern concentration. Bishop was entranced. He stood up in his chair, watching them, his head hanging forward as if any moment it might drop off. Tarwater, his eyes dark and distant, stared through them. They might have been insects buzzing across the surface of his vision.

When the music whined to a stop, they clambered back to their table and sprawled in their chairs. Rayber turned his hearing aid on and winced as Bishop's bellow blared into his head. The child was jumping up and down in his chair, roaring his disappointment. As soon as the dancers saw him, he stopped making the noise and stood still, devouring them with his gape. An angry silence fell over them. Their look was shocked and affronted as if they had been betrayed by a fault in creation, something that should have been corrected before they were allowed to see it. With pleasure Rayber could have dashed across the room and swung his lifted chair in their faces. They got up and pushed each other out sullenly, packed themselves in a topless automobile and roared off, sending an indignant spray of gravel against the side of the lodge. Rayber let out his breath as if it were sharp and might cut him. Then his eyes fell on Tarwater.

The boy was looking directly at him with an omniscient smile, faint but decided. It was a smile that Rayber had seen on his face before. It seemed to mock him from an ever-deepening inner knowledge that grew in indifference as it came nearer and nearer to a secret truth about him. Without warning its meaning pierced Rayber and he felt such a fury that for the moment all his strength left him. Go, he wanted to shout. Get your damn impudent face out of my sight! Go to hell! Go baptize the whole world!

The woman had been standing for some time at his side, waiting to take their order but she could have been invisible for all the notice he paid her. She began tapping the menu on a glass, then she slid it in front of his face. Without reading it, he said, "Three hamburger plates," and thrust it aside.

When she was gone, he said in a dry voice, "I want to lay some cards on the table." He sought the boy's eyes and steadied himself by the hated glint in them.

Tarwater looked at the table as if waiting for the cards to be laid on it.

"That means I want to talk straight to you," Rayber said, rigidly keeping the exasperation out of his voice. He strove to make his gaze, his tone, as indifferent as his listener's "I have some things to say to you that you'll have to listen to. What you do about what I have to say is your own business. I have no further interest in telling you what to do. I only intend to put the facts before you." His voice was thin and brittle-sounding. He might have been reading from a paper. "I notice that you've begun to be able to look Bishop in the eye. That's good. It means you're making progress but you needn't think that because you can look him in the eye now, you've saved yourself from what's preying on you. You haven't. The old man still has you in his grip. Don't think he hasn't."

The boy continued to give him the same omniscient look. "It's you the seed fell in," he said. "It ain't a thing you can do about it. It fell on bad ground but it fell in deep. With me," he said proudly, "it fell on rock and the wind carried it away."

The schoolteacher grasped the table as if he were going to push it forward into the boy's chest. "Goddam you!" he said in a breathless harsh voice. "It fell in us both alike. The difference is that I know it's in me and I keep it under control. I weed it out but you're too blind to know it's in you. You don't even know what makes you do the things you do."

The boy looked at him angrily but he said nothing.

At least, Rayber thought, I've shocked that look off his face. He did not say anything for a few moments while he thought how to continue.

The woman returned with the three plates. She set them down slowly, giving herself time for observation. The man's face had a sweaty harassed look and so did the boy's. He threw her an ugly glance. The man began to eat at once as if he wanted to get it over with. The little boy took his bun apart and began to lick the mustard off it. The other boy looked at his as if it were probably bad meat and did not touch it. She left and watched indignantly for a few seconds from the kitchen door. The boy finally picked his hamburger up. He raised it half-way to his mouth and then put it down again. He picked it up and put it down twice without biting into it. Then he pulled his hat down and sat there, his arms folded. She had had enough and closed the door.

The schoolteacher leaned forward across the table, his eyes pin-pointed and very bright. "You can't eat," he said, "because something is eating you. And I intend to tell you what it is."

"Worms," the boy hissed as if his disgust could not be contained an instant longer.

"It takes guts to listen," Rayber said.

Tarwater leaned toward him with a kind of blaring attention. "You ain't got nothing to say to me that I don't have the guts to listen to," he said.

The schoolteacher sat back. "All right," he said, "then listen." He folded his arms and looked at him for an instant before he began. Then he started coldly. "The old man told you to baptize Bishop. You have that order lodged in your head like a boulder blocking your path."

The blood drained from the boy's face but his eyes did not swerve. They looked at Rayber furiously, the glint in them gone.

The schoolteacher spoke slowly, picking his words as if he were looking for the steadiest stones to step on across a rushing stream. "Until you get rid of this compulsion to baptize Bishop, you'll never make any progress toward being a normal person. I said in the boat you were going to be a freak. I shouldn't have said that. I only meant you had the choice. I want you to see the choice. I want you to make the choice and not simply be driven by a compulsion you don't understand. What we understand, we can control," he said. "You have to understand what it is that blocks you. I wonder if you're smart enough to take this in. It's not simple."

The boy's face seemed dry and old as if he had taken it in long ago, and now it was part of him like the current of death in his blood. The schoolteacher was touched by this muteness before the facts. His anger left him. The room was silent. A pink cast had fallen from the windows over the table. Tarwater looked away from his uncle at Bishop. The little boy's hair was pink and lighter than his face. He was sucking his spoon; his eyes were drowned in silence.

"I want to put two solutions before you," Rayber said. "What you do is up to you."

Tarwater looked at him again, with no mockery, no glint in his eye, but with no anticipation either, as if his course were irrevocably set.

"Baptism is only an empty act," the schoolteacher said. "If there's any way to be born again, it's a way that you accomplish yourself, an understanding about yourself that you reach after a long time, perhaps a long effort. It's nothing you get from above by spilling a little water and a few words. What you want to do is meaningless, so the easiest solution would be simply to do it. Right here now, with this glass of water. I would permit it in order to get it out of your mind. As far as I'm concerned, you may baptize him at once." He pushed his own glass of water across the table. His look was patient and ironical.

The boy's glance touched the top of the glass and then bounded off. His hand lying by the side of his plate twitched. He jammed it into his pocket and looked the other way, out the window. His whole aspect seemed shaken as if his integrity had been dangerously challenged.

The schoolteacher pulled back the glass of water. "I knew that would be too cheap for you," he said. "I knew you would refuse to do anything so unworthy of the courage you've already shown." He raised the glass and drank the rest of the water. Then he set it down on the table. He looked tired enough to collapse; his aspect was so weary that he might just have attained the top of a mountain he had been climbing for days.

After an interval he said, "The other way is not so simple. It's the way I've chosen for myself. It's the way you take as a result of being born again the natural way—through your own efforts. Your intelligence." His words had a disconnected sound. "The other way is simply to face it and fight it, to cut down the weed every time you see it appear. Do I have to tell you this? An intelligent boy like you?"

"You don't have to tell me nothing," Tarwater murmured.

"I don't have a compulsion to baptize him," Rayber

said. "My own is more complicated, but the principle is the same. The way we have to fight it is the same."

"It ain't the same," Tarwater said. He turned toward his uncle. The glint had reappeared. "I can pull it up by the roots, once and for all. I can do something. I ain't like you. All you can do is think what you would have done if you had done it. Not me. I can do it. I can act." He was looking at his uncle now with a completely fresh contempt. "It's nothing about me like you," he said.

"There are certain laws that determine every man's conduct," the schoolteacher said. "You are no exception." He saw with perfect clarity that the only feeling he had for this boy was hate. He loathed the very sight of him.

"Wait and see," Tarwater said as if it needed only a short time to be proved.

"Experience is a terrible teacher," Rayber said.

The boy shrugged and got up. He walked off, across the room to the screen door where he stood looking out. At once Bishop climbed down off his chair and started after him, putting on his hat as he went. Tarwater stiffened when the child approached but he did not move and Rayber watched as the two of them stood there side by side, looking out the door —the two figures, hatted and somehow ancient, bound together by some necessity of nerve that excluded him. He was startled to see the boy put his hand on Bishop's neck just under his hat, open the door and guide him out of it. It occurred to him that what he meant by "doing something" was to make a slave of the child. Bishop would be at his command like a faithful dog. Instead of avoiding him, he planned to control him, to show who was master.

And I will not permit that, he said. If anyone controlled Bishop, it would be himself. He put his money on the table under the salt-shaker and went out after them.

The sky was a bright pink, casting such a weird light that every color was intensified. Each weed that grew out of the gravel looked like a live green nerve. The world might have been shedding its skin. The two were in front of him half way down the dock, walking slowly, Tarwater's hand still resting just under Bishop's hat; but it seemed to Rayber that it was Bishop who was doing the leading, that the child had made the capture. He thought with a grim pleasure that sooner or later the boy's confidence in his own judgment would be brought low.

When they arrived at the end of the dock, they stood looking down into the water. Then to Rayber's chagrin, the boy lifted the child like a sack under the arms and lowered him over the edge of the dock into the boat that was tied there.

"I haven't given you permission to take Bishop out in the boat," Rayber said.

Tarwater may have heard or he may not; he did not answer. He sat down on the edge of the dock and for a few moments looked across the water at the opposite bank. Part of a red globe hung almost motionless in the far side of the lake as if it were the other end of the elongated sun cut through the middle by a swath of forest. Pink and salmon-colored clouds floated in the water at different depths. Suddenly Rayber wanted nothing so much as a half hour to himself, without sight of either of them. "But you may take him," he said, "if you'll be careful."

The boy didn't move. He was leaning forward, his thin shoulders hunched, his hands gripped on the edge of the dock. He seemed poised there waiting to make a momentous move.

He dropped down into the boat with Bishop.

"You'll look after him?" Rayber asked.

Tarwater's face was like a very old mask, colorless and dry. "I'll tend to him," he said.

"Thanks," his uncle said. He experienced a short feeling of warmth for the boy. He strolled back down the dock to the lodge and when he reached the door, he turned and watched the boat move out into view on the lake. He raised his arm and waved but Tarwater showed no sign of seeing him and Bishop's back was turned. The small black-hatted figure sat like a passenger being borne by the surly oarsman across the lake to some mysterious destination.

Back in his room, Rayber lay on the cot trying to feel the release he had felt when he started out in the car in the afternoon. More than anything else, what he experienced in the boy's presence was the feeling of pressure and when it was taken off for a while, he

realized how intolerable it was. He lay there thinking
with distaste of the moment when the silent mutinous
face would appear again in the door. He imagined
the rest of the summer spent coping with the boy's
cold intractability. He began to consider the pos-
sibility of his leaving of his own accord and after a
moment he knew that this was actually what he
wanted him to do. He no longer felt any challenge to
rehabilitate him. All he wanted now was to get rid of
him. He thought with horror of being stuck with him
for good and began to consider ways that he might
hasten his departure. He knew he would never leave
as long as Bishop was around. The thought flew
through his mind that he might put Bishop in an institution for a few weeks. He was shaken and turned
his mind to other things. For a while he dozed and
dreamed that he and Bishop were speeding away in
the car, escaping safely from a lowering tornado-like
cloud. He awoke to find the room growing dim.

He got up and went to the window. The boat with
the two of them in it was near the middle of the lake,
almost still. They were sitting there facing each other
in the isolation of the water, Bishop small and squat,
and Tarwater gaunt, lean, bent slightly forward, his
whole attention concentrated on the opposite figure.
They seemed to be held still in some magnetic field
of attraction. The sky was an intense purple as if it
were about to explode into darkness.

Rayber left the window and threw himself on the
cot again but he was no longer sleepy. He had a pe-

culiar sense of waiting, of marking time. He lay with his eyes closed as if listening to something he could hear only when his hearing aid was off. He had had this sense of waiting, kin in degree but not in kind, when he was a child and expected any moment that the city would blossom into an eternal Powderhead. Now he sensed that he waited for a cataclysm. He waited for all the world to be turned into a burnt spot between two chimneys.

All he would be was an observer. He waited with serenity. Life had never been good enough to him for him to wince at its destruction. He told himself that he was indifferent even to his own dissolution. It seemed to him that this indifference was the most that human dignity could achieve, and for the moment forgetting his lapses, forgetting even his narrow escape of the afternoon, he felt he had achieved it. To feel nothing was peace.

He watched idly as a round red moon rose into the lower corner of his window. It might have been the sun rising on the upsidedown half of the world. He came to a decision. When the boy came back he would say: Bishop and I are returning to town tonight. You may go with us under these conditions: not that you *begin* to cooperate, but that you cooperate, fully and completely, that you change your attitude, that you allow yourself to be tested, that you prepare yourself to enter school in the fall, and that you take that hat off your head right now and throw it out the window into the lake. If you can't meet these requirements, then Bishop and I are leaving by ourselves.

It had taken him five days to reach this state of clarity. He thought of his foolish emotions the night the boy had come, thought of himself sitting by the side of the bed, thinking that at last he had a son with a future. He saw himself again following the boy down back alleys to end finally at a detestable temple, saw the idiot figure of himself standing with his head in the window, listening to the mad child preach. It was unbelievable. Even the plan to take the boy back to Powderhead seemed ridiculous to him now and going to Powderhead this afternoon was the act of an insane person. His indecision, his uncertainty, his eagerness up to now appeared shameful and absurd to him. He felt that he had regained his senses after five days of madness. He could not wait for them to return so that he could deliver his ultimatum.

He closed his eyes and went over the scene in detail, seeing the sullen face at bay, the haughty eyes forced to look down. His power would lie in the fact that he was indifferent now whether the boy stayed or went, or not indifferent for he positively wanted him to leave. He smiled at the thought that his indifference lacked that one perfection. Presently he dozed again, and again he and Bishop were fleeing in the car, the tornado just behind them.

When he awoke again, the moon travelling toward the middle of the window had lost its color. He sat up startled as if it were a face looking in on him, a pale messenger breathlessly arrived.

He got up and went to the window and leaned out. The sky was a hollow black and an empty road of moonlight crossed the lake. He leaned far out, his eyes narrowed, but he could see nothing. The stillness disturbed him. He turned the hearing aid on and at once his head buzzed with the steady drone of crickets and treefrogs. He searched for the boat in the darkness and could see nothing. He waited expectantly. Then an instant before the cataclysm, he grabbed the metal box of the hearing aid as if he were clawing his heart. The quiet was broken by an unmistakable bellow.

He did not move. He remained absolutely still, wooden, expressionless, as the machine picked up the sounds of some fierce sustained struggle in the distance. The bellow stopped and came again, then it began steadily, swelling. The machine made the sounds seem to come from inside him as if something in him were tearing itself free. He clenched his teeth. The muscles in his face contracted and revealed lines of pain beneath harder than bone. He set his jaw. No cry must escape him. The one thing he knew, the one thing he was certain of was that no cry must escape him.

The bellow rose and fell, then it blared out one last time, rising out of its own momentum as if it were escaping finally, after centuries of waiting, into silence. The beady night noises closed in again.

He remained standing woodenly at the window. He knew what had happened. What had happened was as plain to him as if he had been in the water with the boy and the two of them together had taken the child and held him under until he ceased to struggle.

He stared out over the empty still pond to the dark wood that surrounded it. The boy would be moving off through it to meet his appalling destiny. He knew with an instinct as sure as the dull mechanical beat of his heart that he had baptized the child even as he drowned him, that he was headed for everything the old man had prepared him for, that he moved off now through the black forest toward a violent encounter with his fate.

He stood there trying to remember something else before he moved away. It came to him finally as something so distant and vague in his mind that it might already have happened, a long time ago. It was that tomorrow they would drag the pond for Bishop.

He stood waiting for the raging pain, the intolerable hurt that was his due, to begin, so that he could ignore it, but he continued to feel nothing. He stood light-headed at the window and it was not until he realized there would be no pain that he collapsed.

THREE

X

THE headlights revealed the boy at the side of the road, slightly crouched, his head turned expectantly, his eyes for an instant lit red like the eyes of rabbits and deer that streak across the highway at night in the path of speeding cars. His pantslegs were wet up to the knees as if he had been through a swamp. The driver, minute in the glassed cab, brought the looming truck to a halt and left the motor idling while he leaned across the empty seat and opened the door. The boy climbed in.

It was an auto-transit truck, huge and skeletal, carrying four automobiles packed in it like bullets.

The driver, a wiry man with a nose sharply twisted down and heavy-lidded eyes, gave the rider a suspicious look and then shifted gears and the truck began to move again, rumbling fiercely. "You got to keep me awake or you don't ride, buddy," he said. "I ain't picking you up to do you a favor." His voice, from some other part of the country, curled at the end of each sentence.

Tarwater opened his mouth as if he expected words to come out of it but none came. He remained, staring at the man, his mouth half-open, his face white.

"I'm not kiddin', kid," the driver said.

The boy kept his elbows gripped into his sides to prevent his frame from shaking. "I only want to go as far as where this road joins 56," he said finally. There were queer ups and downs in his voice as if he were using it for the first time after some momentous failure. He appeared to listen to it himself, to be trying to hear beyond the quaver in it to some solid basis of sound.

"Start talking," the driver said.

The boy wet his lips. After a moment he said in a high voice, entirely out of control, "I never wasted my life talking. I always done something."

"What you done lately?" the man asked. "How come your pantslegs are wet?"

He looked down at his wet pantslegs and kept looking. They seemed to turn his mind entirely from what he had been going to say, to absorb his attention completely.

"Wake up, buddy," the driver said. "I say how come are your pantslegs wet?"

"Because I never took them off when I done it," he said. "I took off my shoes but I never taken off my pants."

"When you done what?"

"I'm going home," he said. "It's a place I get off at on 56 and then down that road a piece I take a dirt road. It's liable to be morning before I get there."

"How come your pantslegs are wet?" the driver persisted.

"I drowned a boy," Tarwater said.

"Just one?" the driver asked.

"Yes." He reached over and caught hold of the sleeve of the man's shirt. His lips worked a few seconds. They stopped and then started again as if the force of a thought were behind them but no words. He shut his mouth, then tried again but no sound came. Then all at once the sentence rushed out and was gone. "I baptized him."

"Huh?" the man said.

"It was an accident. I didn't mean to," he said breathlessly. Then in a calmer voice he said, "The words just come out of themselves but it don't mean nothing. You can't be born again."

"Make sense," the man said.

"I only meant to drown him," the boy said. "You're only born once. They were just some words that run out of my mouth and spilled in the water." He shook his head violently as if to scatter his thoughts.

"There's nothing where I'm going but the stall," he began again, "because the house is burnt up but that's the way I want it. I don't want nothing of his. Now it's all mine."

"Of his whose?" the man muttered.

"Of my great-uncle's," the boy said. "I'm going back there. I ain't going to leave it again. I'm in full charge there. No voice will be uplifted. I shouldn't never have left it except I had to prove I wasn't no prophet and I've proved it." He paused and jerked the man's sleeve. "I proved it by drowning him. Even if I did baptize him that was only an accident. Now all I have to do is mind my own bidnis until I die. I don't have to baptize or prophesy."

The man only looked at him, shortly, and then back at the road.

"It's not going to be any destruction or any fire," the boy said. "There are them that can act and them that can't, and them that are hungry and them that ain't. That's all. I can act. And I ain't hungry." The words crowded out as if they were pushing each other forward. Then he was suddenly silent. He seemed to watch the darkness that the headlights pushed in front of them, always at the same distance. Sudden signs would spring up and vanish at the side of the road.

"That don't make sense but make up some more of it," the driver said. "I gotta stay awake. I ain't riding you just for a good time."

"I don't have no more to say," Tarwater said. His

voice was thin, as if many more words would destroy it permanently. It seemed to break off after each sound had found its way out. "I'm hungry," he said.

"You just said you weren't hungry," the driver said.

"I ain't hungry for the bread of life," the boy said. "I'm hungry for something to eat here and now. I threw up my dinner and I didn't eat no supper."

The driver began to feel in his pocket. He pulled out half a bent sandwich wrapped in waxed paper. "You can have this," he said. "It don't have but one bite out of it. I didn't like it."

Tarwater took it and held it wrapped in his hand. He didn't open it.

"Okay, eat it!" the driver said in an exasperated voice. "What's the matter with you?"

"When I come to eat, I ain't hungry," Tarwater said. "It's like being empty is a thing in my stomach and it don't allow nothing else to come down in there. If I ate it, I would throw it up."

"Listen," the driver said, "I don't want you puking in here and if you got something catching, you get out right now."

"I'm not sick," the boy said. "I never been sick in my life except sometimes when I over ate myself. When I baptized him it wasn't nothing but words. Back home," he said, "I'll be in charge. I'll have to sleep in the stall until I get to where I can build me back a house. If I hadn't been a big fool I'd have taken him out and burned him up outside. I wouldn't have burned up the house along with him."

"Live and learn," the driver said.

"My other uncle knows everything," the boy said, "but that don't keep him from being a fool. He can't do nothing. All he can do is figure it out. He's got this wired head. There's an electric cord runs into his ear. He can read your mind. He knows you can't be born again. I know everything he knows, only I can do something about it. I did," he added.

"Can't you talk about something else?" the driver asked. "How many sisters you got at home?"

"I was born in a wreck," the boy said.

He took off his hat and rubbed his head. His hair was flat and thin, dark across his white forehead. He held the hat in his lap like a bowl and looked into it. He took out a box of wooden matches and a white card. "I put all this here in my hat when I drowned him," he said. "I was afraid my pockets would get wet." He held up the card close to his eyes and read it aloud. "T. Fawcett Meeks. Southern Copper Parts. Mobile, Birmingham, Atlanta." He stuck the card in the inside band of his hat and put the hat back on his head. He put the box of matches in his pocket.

The driver's head was beginning to roll. He shook it and said, "Talk, dammit."

The boy reached into his pocket and pulled out the combination corkscrew-bottleopener the school-teacher had given him. "My uncle give me this," he said. "He ain't so bad. He knows a heap. I speck I'll be able to use this thing some time or other," and he looked at it lying compact in the center of his hand. "I speck it'll come in handy," he said, "to open something."

"Tell me a joke," the driver said.

The boy didn't look as if he knew any joke. He didn't look as if he knew what a joke was. "Do you know what the greatest invention of man is?" he asked finally.

"Naw," the driver said, "what?"

He didn't answer. He was staring ahead again into the darkness and seemed to have forgotten the question.

"What's the greatest invention of man?" the truck driver asked irritably.

The boy turned and looked at him without comprehension. There was a choking sound in his throat and then he said, "What?"

The driver glared a him. "What's the matter with you?"

"Nothing," the boy said. "I feel hungry but I ain't."

"You belong in the booby hatch," the driver muttered. "You ride through these states and you see they all belong in it. I won't see nobody sane again until I get back to Detroit."

For a few miles they rode in silence. The truck moved slower and slower. The driver's lids would fall as if they were weighted with lead and he would shake his head to open them. Almost at once they would close again. The truck began to veer. He shook his head once violently and pulled off the road onto a wide shoulder and leaned back and began to snore without once looking at Tarwater.

The boy sat quietly on his side of the cab. His eyes were open wide without the least look of sleep in them. They seemed not to be able to close but to be open forever on some sight that would never leave them. Presently they closed but his body did not relax. He sat rigidly upright, a still alert expression on his face as if under the closed lids an inner eye were watching, piercing out the truth in the distortion of his dream.

They were sitting facing each other in a boat suspended on a soft bottomless darkness only a little heavier than the black air around them, but the darkness was no hindrance to his sight. He saw through it as if it were day. He looked through the blackness and saw perfectly the light silent eyes of the child across from him. They had lost their diffuseness and were trained on him, fish-colored and fixed. By his side, standing like a guide in the boat, was his faithful friend, lean, shadow-like, who had counseled him in both country and city.

Make haste, he said. Time is like money and money is like blood and time turns blood to dust.

The boy looked up into his friend's eyes, bent upon him, and was startled to see that in the peculiar darkness, they were violet-colored, very close and intense, and fixed on him with a peculiar look of hunger and attraction. He turned his head away, unsettled by their attention.

No finaler act than this, his friend said. In dealing with the dead you have to act. There's no mere word sufficient to say NO.

Bishop took off his hat and threw it over the side where it floated right-side-up, black on the black surface of the lake. The boy turned his head, following the hat with his eyes, and saw suddenly that the bank loomed behind him, not twenty yards away, silent, like the brow of some leviathan lifted just above the surface of the water. He felt bodiless as if he were nothing but a head full of air, about to tackle all the dead.

Be a man, his friend counseled, be a man. It's only one dimwit you have to drown.

The boy edged the boat toward a dark clump of bushes and tied it. Then he removed his shoes, put the contents of his pockets into his hat and put the hat into one shoe, while all the time the grey eyes were fixed on him as if they were waiting serenely for a struggle already determined. The violet eyes, fixed on him also, waited with a barely concealed impatience.

This is no time to dwaddle, his mentor said. Once it's done, it's done forever.

The water slid out from the bank like a broad black tongue. He climbed out of the boat and stood still, feeling the mud between his toes and the wet clinging around his legs. The sky was dotted with fixed tranquil eyes like the spread tail of some celestial night bird. While he stood there gazing, for the moment lost, the child in the boat stood up, caught him around the neck and climbed onto his back. He clung there like a large crab to a twig and the startled boy felt himself sinking backwards into the water as if the whole bank were pulling him down.

Sitting upright and rigid in the cab of the truck, his muscles began to jerk, his arms flailed, his mouth opened to make way for cries that would not come. His pale face twitched and grimaced. He might have been Jonah clinging wildly to the whale's tongue.

The silence in the truck was corrugated with the snores of the driver, whose head rolled from side to side. The boy's jerking arms almost touched him once or twice as he struggled to extricate himself from a monstrous enclosing darkness. Occasionally a car would pass, illuminating for an instant his contorted face. He grappled with the air as if he had been flung like a fish on the shores of the dead without lungs to breathe there. The night finally began to fade. A plateau of red appeared in the eastern sky just above the treeline and a dun-colored light began to reveal the fields on either side. Suddenly in a high raw voice the defeated boy cried out the words of baptism, shuddered, and opened his eyes. He heard the sibilant oaths of his friend fading away on the darkness.

He sat trembling in the corner of the cab, exhausted, dizzy, holding his arms tight against his sides. The plateau had widened and was broken by the sun which rose through it majestically with a long red wingspread. With his eyes open, his face began to look less alert. Deliberately, forcefully, he closed the inner eye that had witnessed his dream.

In his hand he was clutching the truck driver's sandwich. His fingers had clenched it through. He loosened them and looked at it as if he had no idea what it was; then he put it in his pocket.

After a second he grabbed the driver's shoulder and shook him violently and the man woke up and grabbed the steering wheel convulsively as if the truck were moving at a high rate of speed. Then he perceived that it was not moving at all. He turned and glared at the boy. "What do you think you're doing in here? Where do you think you're going?" he asked in an enraged voice.

Tarwater's face was pale but determined. "I'm going home," he said. "I'm in charge there now."

"Well get out and go then," the driver said. "I don't ride nuts in the day time."

With dignity the boy opened the door and stepped down out of the cab. He stood, scowling but aloof, by the side of the road and waited until the gigantic monster had grated away and disappeared. The highway stretched in front of him, lean and grey, and he began to walk, putting his feet down hard on the ground. His legs and his will were good enough. He set his face toward the clearing. By sundown he would be there, by sundown he would be where he could begin to live his life as he had elected it, and where, for the rest of his days, he would make good his refusal.

XI

AFTER he had walked about an hour, he took out the truck driver's pierced sandwich which he had stuck, still wrapped, in his pocket. He undid it and let the paper blow behind. The truck driver had bitten off one of the pointed ends. The boy put the unbitten end in his mouth but after a second he took it out again with faint teeth marks in it and put it back in his pocket. His stomach alone rejected it; his face looked violently hungry and disappointed.

The morning had opened up, clear and cloudless and brilliant. He walked on the embankment and did not look over his shoulder as cars came behind him and swiftly passed, but as each one disappeared on the narrowing strip of highway, he felt the distance between himself and his goal grow longer. The ground under him was strange to his feet, as if he were walking on the back of a giant beast which might any moment stretch a muscle and send him rolling into the ditch below. The sky was like a fence of light to keep it in. The glare forced him to lower his lids but on the other side of it, hidden from his daily sight but present to his inner eye that remained rigidly open, there stretched the clear grey borders of the country he had saved himself from crossing into.

He repeated every few yards, to force himself on faster, that he would soon be home, that there was only the rest of the day between him and the clearing. His throat and eyes burned with dryness and his bones felt brittle as if they belonged to a person older than himself and with much experience; and when he considered it—his experience—it was apparent to him that since his great-uncle's death, he had lived the lifetime of a man. It was as no boy that he returned. He returned tried in the fire of his refusal, with all the old man's fancies burnt out of him, with all the old man's madness smothered for good, so that there was never any chance it would break out in him. He had saved himself forever from the fate he had envisioned when, standing in the school-teacher's hall and looking into the eyes of the dim-witted child, he had seen himself trudging off into the distance in the bleeding stinking mad shadow of Jesus, lost forever to his own inclinations.

The fact that he had actually baptized the child disturbed him only intermittently and each time he thought of it, he reviewed its accidental nature. It was an accident and nothing more. He considered only that the boy was drowned and that he had done it, and that in the order of things, a drowning was a more important act than a few words spilled in the water. He realized that in this small instance the schoolteacher had succeeded where he had failed. The schoolteacher had not baptized him. He recalled his words: "My guts are in my head." My guts are in my head too, the boy thought. Even if by some chance it had not been an accident, what was of no consequence in the first place was of no consequence in the second; and he had succeeded in drowning the child. He had not said NO, he had done it.

The sun, from being only a ball of glare, was becoming distinct like a large pearl, as if sun and moon had fused in a brilliant marriage. The boy's narrowed eyes made a black spot of it. When he was a child he had several times, experimentally, commanded the sun to stand still, and once for as long as he watched it—a few seconds—it had stood still, but when he turned his back, it had moved. Now he would have liked for it to get out of the sky altogether or to be veiled in a cloud. He turned his face enough to rid his vision of it and was aware again of the country which seemed to lie beyond the silence, or in it, stretching off into the distance around him.

Quickly he set his mind again on the clearing. He thought of the burnt spot in the center of it and he imagined with a careful deliberateness how he would pick up any burnt bone that he might find in the ashes of the house and sling it off into the nearest gulley. He envisioned the calm and detached person who would do this, who would clear out the rubble and build back the house. Beyond the glare, he was aware of another figure, a gaunt stranger, the ghost who had been born in the wreck and who had fancied himself destined at that moment to the torture of prophecy. It was apparent to the boy that this person, who paid him no attention, was mad.

As the sun burned brighter, he became more and more thirsty and his hunger and thirst combined in a pain that shot up and down him and across from shoulder to shoulder. He was about to sit down when ahead in a brush-swept space off the side of the road he saw a Negro's shack. A small colored boy stood in the yard, alone except for a razor-backed shoat. His eyes were already fixed on the boy coming down the road. As Tarwater came nearer he saw a cluster of colored children watching him from the shack door. There was a well to the side under a sugarberry tree and he quickened his pace.

"I want me some water," he said, approaching the forward boy. He took the sandwich from his pocket and handed it to him. The child, who was about the size and shape of Bishop, put it to his mouth with the same motion that he took it and never removed his eyes from the boy's face.

"Yonder hit," he said and pointed with the sandwich to the well.

Tarwater went to it and cranked the bucket up level with the rim. There was a dipper but he did not use it. He leaned over and put his face to the water and drank. He drank until he began to feel dizzy. Then he pulled off his hat and thrust his head into the water. As it touched the deeper parts of his face, a shock ran through him, as if he had never been touched by water before. He looked down into a grey clear pool, down and down to where two silent serene eyes were gazing at him. He tore his head away from the bucket and stumbled backwards while the blurred shack, then the hog, then the coloured child, his eyes still fixed on him, came into focus. He slammed his hat down on his wet head and wiped his sleeve across his face and walked hastily away. The little Negroes watched him until he was off the place and had disappeared down the highway.

The vision stuck like a burr in his head and it took him more than a mile to realize he had not seen it. The water had strangely not assuaged his thirst. To take his mind off it, he reached in his pocket and pulled out the schoolteacher's present and began to admire it. It reminded him that he also had a nickel. The first store or filling station he came to, he would buy himself a drink and open it with the opener. The little instrument glittered in the center of his palm as if it promised to open great things for him. He began to realize that he had not adequately appreciated the schoolteacher while he had the opportunity. The lines of his uncle's face had already become less precise in his mind and he began to see again the eyes shadowed with knowledge that he had imagined before he went to the city. He returned the corkscrew-bottleopener to his pocket and held it there in his hand as if henceforth it would be his talisman.

Presently up ahead, he caught sight of the crossroads where 56 joined the highway he was on. The dirt road was not ten miles down from this point. There was a patched-together store and filling station on the far side of the crossroad. He hastened on in anticipation of the drink he was going to buy, his thirst growing by the second. Then as he came closer, he saw the large woman who stood in the door of the place. His thirst increased but his enthusiasm fled. She was leaning against the frame, her arms folded, and she filled almost the whole entrance. She was a black-eyed woman with a granite-like face and a tongue persistent to question. He and his great-uncle had traded at this place on occasion and when the woman was there, the old man had liked to linger and discourse, for he found her as pleasant as a shade tree. The boy had always stood by impatiently, kicking up the gravel, his face dark with boredom.

She spotted him across the highway and although

she did not move or raise her hand, he could feel her eyes reeling him in. He crossed the highway and was drawn forward, scowling at a neutral space between her chin and shoulder. After he had arrived and stopped, she did not speak but only looked at him and he was obliged to direct a glance upward at her eyes. They were fixed on him with a black penetration. There was all knowledge in her stony face and the fold of her arms indicated a judgment fixed from the foundations of time. Huge wings might have been folded behind her without seeming strange.

"The niggers told me how you done," she said. "It shames the dead."

The boy pulled himself together to speak. He was conscious that no sass would do, that he was called upon by some force outside them both to answer for his freedom and make bold his acts. A tremor went through him. His soul plunged deep within itself to hear the voice of his mentor at its most profound depths. He opened his mouth to overwhelm the woman and to his horror what rushed from his lips, like the shriek of a bat, was an obscenity he had overheard once at a fair. Shocked, he saw the moment lost.

The woman did not move a muscle. Presently she said, "And now you come back. And who is going to hire out a boy who burns down houses?"

Still aghast at his failure, he said in a shaky voice, "I ain't ast nobody to hire me out."

"And shames the dead?"

"The dead are dead and stay that way," he said, gaining a little strength.

"And scorns the Resurrection and the Life?"

His thirst was like a rough hand clenched in his throat. "Sell me a purple drink," he said hoarsely.

The woman did not move.

He turned and went, his look as dark as hers. There were circles under his eyes and his skin seemed to have shrunk on the frame of his bones from dryness. The obscenity echoed sullenly in his head. The boy's mind was too fierce to brook impurities of such a nature. He was intolerant of unspiritual evils and with those of the flesh he had never truckled. He felt his victory sullied by the remark that had come from his mouth. He thought of turning and going back and flinging the right words at her but he had still not found them. He tried to think of what the schoolteacher would have said to her but no words of his uncle's would rise to his mind.

The sun was behind him now and his thirst had reached the point where it could not get worse. The inside of his throat felt as if it were coated with burning sand. He moved on doggedly. No cars were passing. He made up his mind that he would flag the next car that passed. He hungered now for companionship as much as food and water. He wanted to explain to someone what he had failed to explain to the woman and with the right words to wipe out the obscenity that had stained his thought.

He had gone almost two more miles when a car

finally passed him and then slowed down and stopped. He had been trudging absently and had not waved it down but when he saw it stop, he began to run forward. By the time he reached it, the driver had leaned over and opened the door. It was a lavender and cream-colored car. The boy scrambled in without looking at the driver and closed the door and they drove on.

Then he turned and looked at the man and an unpleasant sensation that he could not place came over him. The person who had picked him up was a pale, lean, old-looking young man with deep hollows under his cheekbones. He had on a lavender shirt and a thin black suit and a panama hat. His lips were as white as the cigaret that hung limply from one side of his mouth. His eyes were the same color as his shirt and were ringed with heavy black lashes. A lock of yellow hair fell across his forehead from under his pushed-back hat. He was silent and Tarwater was silent. He drove at a leisurely rate and presently he turned in the seat and gave the boy a long personal look. "Live around here?" he asked.

"Not on this road," Tarwater said. His voice was cracked from dryness.

"Going somewheres?"

"To where I live," the boy croaked. "I'm in charge there now."

The man said nothing else for a few minutes. The window by the boy's side was cracked and patched with a piece of adhesive tape and the handle to lower it had been removed. There was a sweet stale odor in the car and there did not seem enough air to breathe freely. Tarwater could see a pale reflection of himself, eyeing him darkly from the window.

"Don't live on this road, huh?" the man said. "Where do your folks live?"

"No folks," Tarwater said. "It's only me. I take care of myself. Nobody tells me what to do."

"Don't huh?" the man said. "I see it's no flies on you."

"No," the boy said, "there's not."

There was something familiar to him in the look of the stranger but he could not place where he had seen him before. The man put his hand in the pocket of his shirt and brought out a silver case. He snapped it open and passed it over to Tarwater. "Smoke?" he said.

The boy had never smoked anything but rabbit tobacco and he did not want a cigaret. He only looked at them.

"Special," the man said, continuing to hold out the case. "You don't get one of this kind every day, but maybe you ain't had much experience smoking."

Tarwater took the cigaret and hung it in the corner of his mouth, exactly as the man's was hung. Out of another pocket, the man produced a silver lighter and flashed the flame over to him. The cigaret didn't light the first time but the second time he pulled in his breath, it lit and his lungs were unpleasantly filled with smoke. The smoke had a peculiar odor.

"Got no folks, huh?" the man said again. "What road do you live on?"

"It ain't even a road to it," the boy said. "I lived with my great-uncle but he's dead, burnt up, and now it's only me." He began to cough violently.

The man reached across the dashboard and opened the glove compartment. Inside, lying on its side was a flat bottle of whiskey. "Help yourself," he said. "It'll kill that cough."

It was an old-looking stamped bottle without the paper front on it and with a bitten-off cork in the top. "I get that special too," the man said. "If there's flies on you, you can't drink it."

The boy grasped the bottle and began to pull at the cork, and simultaneously there came into his head all his great-uncle's warnings about poisonous liquor, all his idiot restrictions about riding with strangers. The essence of all the old man's foolishness flooded his mind like a rising tide of irritation. He grasped the bottle the more firmly and pulled at the cork, which was too far in, with his fingers. He put the bottle between his knees and took the schoolteacher's corkscrew-bottleopener out of his pocket.

"Say, that's nifty," the man said.

The boy smiled. He pushed the corkscrew in the cork and pulled it out. Never a thought of the old man's but he would change it now. "This here thing will open anything," he said.

The stranger was driving slowly, watching him.

He lifted the bottle to his lips and took a long swallow. The liquid had a deep barely concealed bitterness that he had not expected and it appeared to be thicker than any whiskey he had ever had before. It burned his throat savagely and his thirst raged anew so that he was obliged to take another and fuller swallow. The second was worse than the first and he perceived that the stranger was watching him with what might be a leer.

"Don't like it, huh?" he said.

The boy felt a little dizzy but he thrust his face forward and said, "It's better than the Bread of Life!" and his eyes glittered.

He sat back and took the cork off the opener and put it back on the bottle and returned the bottle to the compartment. Already his motions seemed to be slowing down. It took him some time to get his hand back in his lap. The stranger said nothing and Tarwater turned his face to the window.

The liquor lay like a hot rock in the pit of his stomach, heating his whole body, and he felt himself pleasantly deprived of responsibility or of the need for any effort to justify his actions. His thoughts were heavy as if they had to struggle up through some dense medium to reach the surface of his mind. He was looking into thick unfenced woods. The car moved almost slow enough for him to count the outside trunks and he began to count them, one, one, one, until they began to merge and flow together. He leaned his head against the glass and his heavy lids closed.

After a few minutes the stranger reached over and pushed his shoulder but he did not stir. The man then began to drive faster. He drove about five miles, speeding, before he espied a turnoff into a dirt road. He took the turn and raced along for a mile or two and then pulled his car off the side of the road and drove down into a secluded declivity near the edge of the woods. He was breathing rapidly and sweating. He got out and ran around the car and opened the other door and Tarwater fell out of it like a loosely-filled sack. The man picked him up and carried him into the woods.

Nothing passed on the dirt road and the sun continued to move with a brilliant blandness on its way. The woods were silent except for an occasional trill or caw. The air itself might have been drugged. Now and then a large silent floating bird would glide into the treetops and after a moment rise again.

In about an hour, the stranger emerged alone and looked furtively about him. He was carrying the boy's hat for a souvenir and also the corkscrew-bottle-opener. His delicate skin had acquired a faint pink tint as if he had refreshed himself on blood. He got quickly into his car and sped away.

When Tarwater woke up, the sun was directly overhead, very small and silver, sifting down light that seemed to spend itself before it reached him. He saw first his thin white legs stretching in front of him. He was propped up against a log that lay across a small open space between two very tall trees. His hands were loosely tied with a lavender handkerchief which his friend had thought of as an exchange for the hat. His clothes were neatly piled by his side. Only his shoes were on him. He perceived that his hat was gone.

The boy's mouth twisted open and to the side as if it were going to displace itself permanently. In a second it appeared to be only a gap that would never be a mouth again. His eyes looked small and seedlike as if while he was asleep, they had been lifted out, scorched, and dropped back into his head. His expression seemed to contract until it reached some point beyond rage or pain. Then a loud dry cry tore out of him and his mouth fell back into place.

He began to tear savagely at the lavender handkerchief until he had shredded it off. Then he got into his clothes so quickly that when he finished he had half of them on backwards and did not notice. He stood staring down at the spot where the displaced leaves showed him to have lain. His hand was already in his pocket bringing out the box of wooden matches. He kicked the leaves together and set them on fire. Then he tore off a pine branch and set it on fire and began to fire all the bushes around the spot until the fire was eating greedily at the evil ground, burning every spot the stranger could have touched. When it was a roaring blaze, he turned and ran, still holding the pine torch and lighting bushes as he went.

He barely noticed when he ran out of the woods

onto the bare red road. It streaked beneath him like fire hardened and only gradually as his breath choked him did he slow down and begin to take his bearings. The sky, the woods on either side, the ground beneath him, came to a halt and the road assumed direction. It swung down between high red embankments and then mounted a flat field plowed to its edges on either side. Off in the distance a shack, sunk a little on one side, seemed to be afloat on the red folds. Down the hill the wooden bridge lay like the skeleton of some prehistoric beast across the stream bed. It was the road home, ground that had been familiar to him since his infancy but now it looked like strange and alien country.

He stood clenching the blackened burnt-out pine bough. Then after a moment he began to move forward again slowly. He knew that he could not turn back now. He knew that his destiny forced him on to a final revelation. His scorched eyes no longer looked hollow or as if they were meant only to guide him forward. They looked as if, touched with a coal like the lips of the prophet, they would never be used for ordinary sights again.

XII

THE broad road began to narrow until it was no more than a rutted rain-washed gulley which disappeared finally into a blackberry thicket. The sun, red and mammoth, was about to touch the treeline. Tarwater paused an instant here. His glance passed over the ripening berries, turned sharply and pierced into the wood which lay dark and dense before him. He drew in his breath and held it a second before he plunged forward, blindly following the faint path that led down through the wood to the clearing. The air was laden with the odor of honeysuckle and the sharper scent of pine but he scarcely recognized what they were. His senses were stunned and his thought too seemed suspended. Somewhere deep in the wood a woodthrush called and as if the sound were a key turned in the boy's heart, his throat began to tighten.

A faint evening breeze had begun to stir. He stepped over a tree fallen across his path and plunged on. A thorn vine caught in his shirt and tore it but he didn't stop. Farther away the woodthrush called again. With the same four formal notes it trilled its grief against the silence. He was heading straight for a gap in the wood where, through a forked birch, the clearing could be seen below, down the long hill and across the field. Always when he and his great-uncle were returning from the road, they would stop there. It had given the old man the greatest satisfaction to look out over the field and in the distance see his house settled between its chimneys, his stall, his lot, his corn. He might have been Moses glimpsing the promised land.

As Tarwater approached the tree, his shoulders were set high and tense. He seemed to be preparing himself to sustain a blow. The tree, forked a few feet from the ground, loomed in his way. He stopped and with a hand on either trunk, he leaned forward through the fork and looked out at an expanse of crimson sky. His gaze, like a bird that flies through fire, faltered and dropped. Where it fell, two chimneys stood like grieving figures guarding the blackened ground between them. His face appeared to shrink as he looked.

He remained motionless except for his hands. They clenched and unclenched. What he saw was what he had expected to see, an empty clearing. The old man's body was no longer there. His dust would not be mingling with the dust of the place, would not be washed by the seeping rains into the field. The wind by now had taken his ashes, dropped them and scattered them and lifted them up again and carried each mote a different way around the curve of the world. The clearing was burned free of all that had ever oppressed him. No cross was there to say that this was ground that the Lord still held. What he looked out upon was the sign of a broken covenant. The place was forsaken and his own. As he looked, his dry lips parted. They seemed to be forced open by a hunger too great to be contained inside him. He stood there open-mouthed, as if he had no further power to move.

He felt a breeze on his neck as light as a breath and he half-turned, sensing that some one stood behind him. A sibilant shifting of air dropped like a sigh into his ear. The boy turned white.

Go down and take it, his friend whispered. It's ours. We've won it. Ever since you first begun to dig the grave, I've stood by you, never left your side, and now we can take it over together, just you and me. You're not ever going to be alone again.

The boy shuddered convulsively. The presence was as pervasive as an odor, a warm sweet body of air encircling him, a violet shadow hanging around his shoulders.

He shook himself free fiercely and grabbed the matches from his pocket and tore off another pine bough. He held the bough under his arm and with a shaking hand struck a match and held it to the needles until he had a burning brand. He plunged this into the lower branches of the forked tree. The flames crackled up, snapping for the drier leaves and rushing into them until an arch of fire blazed upward. He walked backwards from the spot pushing the torch into all the bushes he was moving away from, until he had made a rising wall of fire between him and the grinning presence. He glared through the flames and his spirits rose as he saw that his adversary would soon be consumed in a roaring blaze. He turned and moved on with the burning brand tightly clenched in his fist.

The path twisted downward through reddened tree trunks that gradually grew darker as the sun sank out of sight. From time to time he plunged the torch into a bush or tree and left it blazing behind him. The wood became less dense. Suddenly it opened and he stood at its edge, looking out on the flat cornfield and far across to the two chimneys. Planes of purpling red above the treeline stretched back like stairsteps to reach the dusk. The corn the old man had left planted was up about a foot and moved in wavering lines of green across the field. It had been freshly plowed. The boy stood there, a small rigid, hatless figure, holding the blackened pine bough.

As he looked, his hunger constricted him anew. It

appeared to be outside him, surrounding him, almost as if it were visible before him, something he could reach out for and not quite touch. He sensed a strangeness about the place as if there might already be an occupant. Beyond the two chimneys, his eyes moved over the stall, grey and weathered, and crossed the back field and stopped at the far black wall of woods. A deep filled quiet pervaded everything. The encroaching dusk seemed to come softly in deference to some mystery that resided here. He stood, leaning slightly forward. He appeared to be permanently suspended there, unable to go forward or back. He became conscious of the very breath he drew. Even the air seemed to belong to another.

Then near the stall he saw a Negro mounted on a mule. The mule was not moving; the two might have been made out of rock. He started forward across the field boldly, raising his fist in a gesture that was half-greeting and half-threat, but after a second his hand opened. He waved and began to run. It was Buford. He would go home with him and eat.

Instantly at the thought of food, he stopped and his muscles contracted with nausea. He blanched with the shock of a terrible premonition. He stood there and felt a crater opening inside him, and stretching out before him, surrounding him, he saw the clear grey spaces of that country where he had vowed never to set foot. Mechanically he began to move forward. He came out on the hard ground of the yard a few feet from the fig tree, but his eyes took the far circuit to it, lingering above the stall and moving beyond it to the far treeline and back. He knew that the next sight to meet his eyes would be the half-dug gaping grave, almost at his feet.

The Negro was watching him steadily. He began to move forward on the mule. When the boy finally forced his eyes to move again, he saw the mule's hooves first and then Buford's feet hanging at its sides. Above, the brown crinkled face was looking down at him with a scorn that could penetrate any surface.

The grave, freshly mounded, lay between them. Tarwater lowered his eyes to it. At its head, a dark rough cross was set starkly in the bare ground. The boy's hands opened stiffly as if he were dropping something he had been clutching all his life. His gaze rested finally on the ground where the wood entered the grave.

Buford said, "It's owing to me he's resting there. I buried him while you were laid out drunk. It's owing to me his corn has been plowed. It's owing to me the sign of his Saviour is over his head."

Nothing seemed alive about the boy but his eyes and they stared downward at the cross as if they followed below the surface of the earth to where its roots encircled all the dead.

The Negro sat watching his strange spent face and grew uneasy. The skin across it tightened as he watched and the eyes, lifting beyond the grave, appeared to see something coming in the distance. Buford turned his head. The darkening field behind him stretched downward toward the woods. When he looked back again, the boy's vision seemed to pierce the very air. The Negro trembled and felt suddenly a pressure on him too great to bear. He sensed it as a burning in the atmosphere. His nostrils twitched. He muttered something and turned the mule around and moved off, across the back field and down to the woods.

The boy remained standing there, his still eyes reflecting the field the Negro had crossed. It seemed to him no longer empty but peopled with a multitude. Everywhere, he saw dim figures seated on the slope and as he gazed he saw that from a single basket the throng was being fed. His eyes searched the crowd for a long time as if he could not find the one he was looking for. Then he saw him. The old man was lowering himself to the ground. When he was down and his bulk had settled, he leaned forward, his face turned toward the basket, impatiently following its progress toward him. The boy too leaned forward, aware at last of the object of his hunger, aware that it was the same as the old man's and that nothing on earth would fill him. His hunger was so great that he could have eaten all the loaves and fishes after they were multiplied.

He stood there, straining forward, but the scene faded in the gathering darkness. Night descended until there was nothing but a thin streak of red between it and the black line of earth but still he stood there. He felt his hunger no longer as a pain but as a tide. He felt it rising in himself through time and darkness, rising through the centuries, and he knew that it rose in a line of men whose lives were chosen to sustain it, who would wander in the world, strangers from that violent country where the silence is never broken except to shout the truth. He felt it building from the blood of Abel to his own, rising and engulfing him. It seemed in one instant to lift and turn him. He whirled toward the treeline. There, rising and spreading in the night, a red-gold tree of fire ascended as if it would consume the darkness in one tremendous burst of flame. The boy's breath went out to meet it. He knew that this was the fire that had encircled Daniel, that had raised Elijah from the earth, that had spoken to Moses and would in the instant speak to him. He threw himself to the ground and with his face against the dirt of the grave, he heard the command. GO WARN THE CHILDREN OF GOD OF THE TERRIBLE SPEED OF MERCY. The words were as silent as seeds opening one at a time in his blood.

When finally he raised himself, the burning bush had disappeared. A line of fire ate languidly at the treeline and here and there a thin crest of flame rose farther back in the woods where a dull red cloud of smoke had gathered. The boy stooped and picked up a handful of dirt off his great-uncle's grave and smeared it on his forehead. Then after a moment, without looking back he moved across the far field and off the way Buford had gone.

By midnight he had left the road and the burning woods behind him and had come out on the highway once more. The moon, riding low above the field beside him, appeared and disappeared, diamond-bright, between patches of darkness. Intermittently the boy's jagged shadow slanted across the road ahead of him as if it cleared a rough path toward his goal. His singed eyes, black in their deep sockets, seemed already to envision the fate that awaited him but he moved steadily on, his face set toward the dark city, where the children of God lay sleeping.